THE WRACKTURN METHOD

A STUDENT TEMPTER'S GUIDE
TO THE SUBVERSION
OF CHRISTIAN HIGHER EDUCATION

Dr. Brian Melton

Moral Apologetics
PRESS

Library of Congress Control Number: 2021935091

ISBN: 978-1-7359363-1-4

POSTHUMOUS PRAISE
FOR THE WRACKTURN METHOD

"If I had only had this handy guide to devilry, I wouldn't have bothered with petty murder."

Cain, son of Adam

"Wrackturn is a wonderful guide to the corruption and enslavement of whole tribes of people. Here, he turns his expert eye to more modern problems. It is more fun than an army of drowned charioteers."

Pharaoh Ramses II

"Incitatus encourages you to read this book. Now. On pain of death."

Emperor Caligula

"A more complete and accurate guide to corrupting the masses in the name of religion cannot be found. Only a step-by-step guide to forced confessions could possibly improve its usefulness."

Tomoas de Torquemada

"Bloody well-written. Suck it dry for all its insights!"

Countess Elizabeth Bathory

"Required reading for any aspiring dictator or secular populist leader who wishes to free his people from the oppressive grip of religious morality."

Maximilien Robespierre

"If Wrackturn hadn't waited so long to publish this text, I would have won at Waterloo."

Napoleon Bonaparte

CONTENTS

PREFACE TO
THE FOREWORD

The slim volume you hold in your hands represents more than a decade and a half of institutional memory and experience of Christian higher education. It also encompasses the observations of faculty and staff that, as I am an historian and this being my bent, I accumulated over the years when people were willing to speak up. In that sense, it also offers the experiences of people better and wiser than I. The central question addressed is simple: How might a flawed but apparently earnest university dedicated to the service of Christ and specifically conscious of the fate of other formerly Christian schools still manage to lose sight of its original mission and finally arrive in a place where it is now (at points) promoting anti-Christian ideals and routinely treating people in un-Christian ways, all in the name of Christ Himself? It is indeed a "three-pipe problem."

Before we go further, I need to clear the air a bit in anticipation of probable boilerplate rejoinders. I am a consistent, principled, politically and culturally conservative Christian in the vein of Francis Schaeffer; I was such a one before the age of Trump and I will remain so afterward. I have never been fired or "abruptly non-renewed" from any job I have ever held. What I talk about in this book is not "fake news." While I've tried to make this interesting and I have adopted a fictional vehicle to do so, virtually everything you read here, even some of the more outlandish things (i.e., university administrators attempting to ban a college textbook because it didn't have pictures), is based on real people, real events, and real issues I have personally observed, or on firsthand, primary source accounts from others.

The main reason I am writing this book is in the hopes of starting a conversation between all concerned—administration, faculty, staff, and students—at a variety of colleges and universities about the ideas it contains. Many schools won't be unlucky enough to allow themselves to get into the state of our fictional Sardis Christian, thankfully including those for whom I currently teach (which are all solid schools that I enjoy and recommend). However, over the years, I have seen more than one faculty member or administrator at even the best of them cast a longing eye toward some of the policies Wrackturn lays out here and the philosophies that produced them. They did this without, I think, fully understanding the implications. I want to expound upon and explain those implications, having seen firsthand what they do to people, to education, and to the cause of Christ. I write this in the hope of saving and, better, *preventing* others from following the path that Wrackturn charts, however tempting that wide and broad way might be. I have no illusions about "fixing" Christian higher ed, but if I can at least make the participants aware of how this has all played out before, perhaps some good can be accomplished.

I therefore want to identify a new avenue of spiritual attack that has obviously proven to be highly effective and is therefore applicable to a broad range of schools and situations. As Wrackturn himself notes later in his preface, evangelicals "are very well defended against the ideas and strategies of two generations ago," but they cannot seem to grasp the threat that is right in front of them. Several schools have taken very clear, strong, and potent measures to guard against infernal stratagems that led to the downfall of Christian education in places like the Ivy League, yet they have been completely blind to the ones that are leading them down a distinct but parallel path that will necessarily end in a similar (if more conservative-ish) destination: the proverbial white-washed tombs full of corruption. I want to expose and explain this new tack as a warning to Christian ministries worldwide so they may guard against it or, if they have already fallen prey to it, repent and return to the narrow path. As just about any child of the 80s can tell you, "Knowing is half the battle."

I also hope that in bringing certain issues out into the open, we can have a frank discussion about the cultures created within the various levels of evangelical education. The fact that I have been so strongly encouraged by others to seek a publisher for this work is testimony to the need for such a conversation. I wanted to share my experience with them to let them know that they are not alone. Many of the people who have been harmed by these cultures are not "bad Christians" for incurring disfavor, whatever they may have been guilt-tripped into believing by a smooth-talking preacher-turned-administrator. What has been done to them is not "just business" and they are not "sinners" for believing themselves and their families to have been ill-used. It doesn't matter at all if "everyone else is doing it." To quote a certain famous preacher whose school is now infamous for how badly it treats its faculty, "If it's Christian, it ought to be better." Such things are *wrong* and they are happening at places loudly claiming to represent Christ *in spite* of the Gospel, *not* because of it.

I am *not* setting out to target any particular group or role in the university system over any other. For example, this is not a tirade aimed at administrators any more than it is at faculty, staff, or students. I find, unfortunately, that when things go this wrong it is usually a group effort (myself regrettably too often included) and there are usually very few completely innocent parties. Therefore, what I am seeking here is to be, for lack of a better description, an "equal opportunity offender." It is my hope that most everyone will find something here to make them feel uncomfortable, then to chuckle at, and in the end to learn from.

Finally, this book is intentionally inspired by the *Screwtape Letters* and I give all credit to C. S. Lewis and his brilliance for creating that particular idiom. I realize there is an obvious risk of seeming unoriginal in this choice; sometimes, as I look around, I'm tempted to ask if there is anyone interested in Christian literature who *hasn't* written a Screwtape Letter or two! I chose this form simply because it fit so well I could hardly avoid it! As I was forced to watch the slow, progressive corruption of Christian education, specifically at a school I was intimately associated with for over a decade, where I had a firsthand view into how it all played out in the faculty and administration, I felt that I could almost see the kinds of designs that Screwtape and Wormwood discussed writ large across the campus with each new shift and each subsequent controversy. Unfortunately, unlike Screwtape and Wormwood, Wrackturn and Nobshank appear to have been so far largely successful and so at this moment, our present story and Lewis's have very different endings indeed. We can pray, however, that it isn't too late to change that outcome.

Brian Melton

March 21, 2021

A note on personalities: While the events and characters in this book were inspired by real life, they are *not* explicit allegories and they do *not* refer directly to any specific person, living or dead. They are intended, instead, to illustrate whole types and classes, not individuals. I claim no inside information about any person and the temptations of various characters are based on my speculations on what *any* person in a similar situation might face, not propositions claiming to describe any one person's specific thoughts or circumstances. For those on their phones in the back of the room: the events and characters in this book are *fictional*.

FOREWORD

I have no intention of explaining how the following book came into my possession. I will admit that it was the result of time spent in places and with people I would rather forget and for which I should probably ask forgiveness. It came to me as a file, wrackturn.dvl, a little-used digital publication format (like a pdf), read-only. The language was one I had never seen before. In what I can only call a providential coincidence, Google Translate identified it as "Oujiangese" and was just then pioneering a since-discontinued beta version that could crack it.

What emerged appears to be an entry-level textbook for a sophomore class at the Tempters Training University—a school for devils. I knew of at least one other now-famous case in recent history when demonic papers have fallen into human hands, so I didn't dismiss the possibility immediately. The book appears to be based on the correspondence of one "Wrackturn," a deputy director, as he oversees the progress of his subordinate, "Nobshank," while they work to corrupt a major Christian university: "Sardis Christian University" and its founding family, the Newritches. The letters apparently take place over the course of an unknown number of years and quite a bit of time may have passed between one and the next. The strategies contained in the letters apparently met with such success that they were later collected and published as a "how-to" guide for up-and-coming fiends assigned to the field of western education.

All of the names appear to be false; in fact, they most probably reside entirely in Wrackturn's fevered imagination. The devils are liars, after all. But, then again, I don't think that affects the accuracy of this book or the efficacy of the "Wrackturn Method" in the least. We could probably insert the name of half a dozen institutions and this book's lessons for their administrations, faculties, and students would be just as important. It's in the hopes of exposing this new and different strategy that I risk offering this text to the world. Times have changed and it appears the devils have changed with them.

PREFACE TO
THE FIFTH EDITION

I t has now been quite some time in the reckoning of the human meatbags since the first edition of this little book was offered to eager students at what was then called the Tempters Training College. When I began this correspondence with Nobshank, I was already confident that much evil would come of it. Our success at Sardis Christian caught the attention of large portions of the lowerarchy, and from there, it was only sensible that the letters should be collected and edited into a form that could be made available to all. Since the first edition, it has been adapted into not only this textbook, but also a movie, an award-winning play, and a first-person shooter available on a variety of platforms.

Evangelical colleges and universities, like so much of American "Christian" subculture, are very well defended against the ideas and strategies of two generations ago. *The Wrackturn Method* represents a radical departure from the traditional approach to corrupting and bamboozling the Enemy's academics, one that I have specially designed to take advantage of the current state of meatbag technology and thinking. It allows the message of Our Father Below to be disseminated to generations of the Enemy's children, using the Enemy's own institutions.

With it, go forth and conquer for Our Father Below! Succeed, and you will taste souls of a vintage you can barely imagine. You know the consequences if you fail.

Yours Infernally,

Wrackturn

His High Excellency, Director of the Supervisor for the Coordinator for the Advancement of Fiendish Excellence

Chief Trustee, Tempters Training University

Professor of Infermetics, Tempters Training University, Third Circle Campus

Professor Emeritus, Department of Doomology, Tempters Training University, Fourth Circle Campus

Provost, Tempters Training University Online

Order of Cthulhu, First Class

Winner of the Anton LaVey Sinister Smile Award

Chairman of the Ouija Oversight and Exploitation Committee

Most Promising Tempter

Etc., Etc.

-1-
Sardis Christian University

My Dear Nobshank,

L et me be the first to congratulate you on your recent promotion to undersecretary. I know you feel it was a long time in coming. Fortunately, given the vacancies created by the sudden "retirement" of the previous deputy director and his team, we now have the opportunity to reward you with a position that may perhaps be more to your liking. We shall see if it is befitting your skill as a tempter or not.

As you know, I have been given considerable latitude by Our Father Below since he appointed me as a deputy director. He has begun an offensive focused on reclaiming the ground lost in recent years, and our own particular part of the front deals with education. Our Father thinks this to be a very important part of the effort, so much so that he created our entire department with just this aim. I am, in turn, now at liberty to entrust you with oversight of our efforts in a key field: Sardis Christian University.

The purpose of my writing to you at this time is to prepare you for the task at hand. You should know from your dossier that SCU is a young school. It was founded by a well-known leader in that movement the little meatbags are calling "Evangelical." You will recall that our previous (very successful) advances into the field of education were being turned back one after the other by a whole cabal of enemy fighters who were bold enough to be dedicated to the idea that their faith was to be believed as a whole and not segregated to any specific part of their lives. I will admit that some of those names still make our oldest tempters, well accustomed to the hottest parts of Hell, break out into cold sweats. You may remember that little Schaeffer fellow, and later on, Plantinga. Then, of course, there was Tolkien; his books are still causing trouble. And Lewis, the dew-beater who somehow got hold of those embarrassing letters. (Thankfully our researchers have managed to marginalize his worst potential for further damage through the tried and true technique of "Popularization." Even though more people are talking about him than ever before, fewer and fewer actually understand him. That happens when we reduce the whole of someone's thought to a bumper sticker, a flip calendar, coffee mug, embroidered pillow, etc., etc., etc.) Unfortunately, these leaders did manage to awaken a sense of the value of education in the little brutes, and one particular man, H. James Newritch, decided to create a system in which a child could pass from birth through a graduate degree entirely under the guidance of teachers influenced by the Enemy's Abominable Book.

You will see at once why Our Father Below cannot tolerate this. If successful, it would not only preserve the potential faith of hundreds or even thousands, it could upset the very delicate balance we've worked so hard to maintain. The education system in the West, such as it is, has been carefully groomed by some of our best tempters to serve as a breeding ground for our kind of thinking. A side effect of the complete self-absorption of secular western—particularly liberal—society is that they have stopped having babies. After all, the little meatbrats are difficult and inconvenient, wholly incompatible with their preferred self-indulgent lifestyle. While we may rejoice at each soulish scream uttered in every abortion and how it deliciously damages all involved—especially the mother and the doctor—it does not do much to advance our agenda into the next generation. Therefore, the liberal domination of the education system means that their worldview can act as a kind of parasite, living on the children of other traditions, and its influence is spread far beyond their own meagre numbers. The fact that most churches have done nothing to inoculate their little ones against this tactic means that we can expect many more years of success with it if we act promptly to eliminate threats such as Sardis Christian University.

For many of their years, we had a tried-and-true tactic that laid low some of their greatest educational strongholds. Using a leftward feinting movement executed subtly over time, we convinced the faculty at these schools that belief in the Enemy's book and, indeed, even the enemy Himself, could not be taken seriously. We marinated the fools in mindless, reflexive rationalism, which promised to give them all the powers and prerogatives of the Enemy Himself but without any of the inconvenience of His morality. Based upon that, we convinced them to "promote" Him out of the picture. We told them, if He existed, He must be far too busy to be concerned with them. This allowed a sort of intellectualized "worship" where they acknowledged the Enemy as a fact without accepting Him as a present reality. Once they could live as if He didn't exist, it was only a short time before they actually began to convince themselves that He was never there at all.

While there were a few weaker-minded faculty who clung to the form of religion, there really was nothing to it. From there, we simply had to play to the prats' sense of tolerance and goodness. You convinced them to accept one apostate onto the faculty to show "how serious we are about fairness and about academic inclusiveness." Then you got them to accept another. And then another. Eventually, once you'd achieved a voting majority, it was a simple matter to have the secular meatbags come out with their real belief that excluding God and a serious view of religion is actually an issue of academic integrity and necessary to maintain the reputation of the university. They would then begin happily excluding the very people who once showed them tolerance—and feel good about it. Why not follow this well-proven approach again, you ask? Sadly, the fact is that historians on the Enemy's side have not been idle. They have analyzed our successes at places like

Harvard, Princeton, Yale, etc., and they've identified both the means and the method of infiltration. Sardis Christian University has already taken steps to try to prevent this by refusing to grant tenure to its faculty. Their thinking is that if a faculty member seems to be drifting, the administration will be able to step in and stifle the dissent preemptively before it has a chance to grow. At first glance, we might think that this is an effective strategy that we ourselves might employ, and it is. But I see in it the seeds of golden opportunity. More on that in future missives.

As you move forward, I expect a full order of battle from the chancellor's office down to the mailroom. Lay this out for me, with commentary on individual personalities and weaknesses. Be sure to establish active communications with all of their tempters via the IMS [infernal messaging system]. You will need instant access to anyone in the structure at all times. This will allow us to not only to identify potential weaknesses and isolate pockets of resistance, but we will be able to single out promising recruits.

Do not, as yet, attach yourself to any particular person or organization within the school. With a younger school such as this, led by a dynamic leader who is constantly pushing things forward to some end or other, it can be difficult to discern exactly what direction things are taking. For the moment, H. James is in good hands with my old associate, Globnobber. As an undersecretary, we want to be sure we connect you to the most effective and influential subject for the school's next generation. I know the waiting might be frustrating—no good tempter enjoys watching others toy with their prey while having none himself—but you can console yourself by remembering how much more powerful your tender ministrations will be when we attach you to your ultimate subject. In the meantime, you can amuse yourself by interfering with parking policies, the telephone system, and cafeteria menus. You might be surprised at the sheer volume of whining and hatred bred if you tweak them properly. Very little seems to bring out human pettiness and rancor more effectively than the idea of having to walk an extra hundred yards or to suddenly discover that "Taco Tuesday" has been rescheduled to

Wednesday.

You suffered much in the gentle care of my predecessor, Nobshank. The fact that you still exist as more than food is a testament to your ingenuity and usefulness. Prove both to me now. I have no greater tolerance for failure than he did.

Yours Infernally,

Wrackturn

-2-
Bent Not Broken

My Dear Nobshank,

I can see from your subtly disrespectful reply that you do not fully appreciate the trust which Our Father Below has placed in me, and I in you. Very well. Allow me to explain this to you in more detail. You have been placed in a position most peculiar in that it offers both ease and the chance to strike a serious blow for the advancement of Hell. Education is a key battleground in general, but it is especially important in undoing the evangelical movement.

Let me begin by refuting your foolish assumption that I am sending you to "destroy" Sardis Christian University. That kind of elementary thinking is what I came to expect from your predecessor. You are indeed correct that "destroying SCU would be almost too easily managed" and that "it is a task that will take me back to my school days." Such a thing would indeed be suited to a junior tempter fresh out of the training univ. All it would take is a few suggestions in the right ears to uncover the long train of sexual misdeeds by any of several administrative leaders or leaking the Newritch family's full financial records or even exploiting the vice president's connection to that particular cult of which he is so fond. If destruction had been our goal, it would have been accomplished long ago.

Our intentions here are much greater and more fiendish. We are not here to *break* SCU, we are here to *bend* it. What we want is a thriving institution that, instead of turning out warriors for the Enemy, creates whole generations of little "Christian" devils who firmly believe themselves to be safely in the Enemy's camp. If we can accomplish this ignoble end, we will have succeeded in making them not only deadly to the church's witness, but willfully impervious to any attempt of the Enemy to reach them. The souls milked as a result of this method will be delicious!

But I am getting ahead of myself. Education, for those without the sight to see, may appear to be a wasted field upon which to expend our efforts. After all, no soul is reclaimed from the Enemy's camp by mere education alone. Why should we expend so much energy on it? There are a number of very good reasons.

First, you must realize that real education is, in practice, a force multiplier in any context and especially so for the meatbags. I think we of the lowerarchy tend to forget that they haven't existed for seemingly endless ages as we have. In all that time, even the most besotted of tempters usually manages to pick up some form of competence. Not so for the bipeds. The Enemy has restricted them to very short lives, at least in the physical world. Every moment of time could be spent in the detailed study of a single subject, and they would die and rot before they have even made a dent in real knowledge. In this sense, it doesn't matter that the Enemy has granted them eternal life, either to wallow in his horrific luminescence or drip torturously into our cups. For key moments in the actual timestream, the ones when they can make real choices, they must start from nothing. Education is really the only option open to them with any hope of overcoming this shortfall. And even we acknowledge the effectiveness of a strong education, as you will remember from your sufferings in the univ.

As a species, they have not a second of their time to waste. Every instant squandered is one lost to them that can never be recovered. As societies (if we can call the putrid networks of social interaction they create for themselves actual "societies"), they can only advance by each generation leaving records of their knowledge to be taught to the next. While it might be amusing to watch them reinvent the wheel while bashing one another over the head with clubs again and again, it is amusement of a sort that quickly becomes dry and boring. It makes for only the dullest and most elementary of sins for consumption. We want refinement, and as ridiculous as their "societies" are, they really do provide us with the best vintages of pained souls. The taste of a hungry man crushing his brother's skull because he put out the fire is nothing compared to the cool, smooth flavor of a death camp commandant. The former burns the throat a bit, perhaps, but the latter lingers on the tongue exquisitely.

What is true for a species is also true for individuals, especially since as their culture advances, none of them have the time to learn exclusively through trial and error. If they want to make their mark, they must enter into an accelerated and intentional period of learning in which each individual reaches out and connects with hundreds of others to benefit from the vicarious experiences of the group. They become little putrid pools into which those who have gone before pour their accumulated knowledge and wisdom. This allows the pitiful meatbags to advance at an alarming rate and to achieve results far beyond what their meager years might suggest could ever be possible. Leave people to their own devices, and they might, on their own natural talents, develop the ability to speak well. Give the same people a good education, connecting them with the greatest human minds of their short history, and they will be able to move stones to weep. As a tempter, which would you rather corrupt?

And finally, while merely having an education may not "save" any of them *from* us, it can save them *for* us. Education, properly corrupted, is a wonderful tool for subtly twisting, turning, bending, breaking, debauching, degrading, and defiling even the most promising of the Enemy's children. If you will take a moment to review our long list of trophies, easily available to you on the Infernet, especially the trophies won since the period our kind have taught their historians to call the "Enlightenment," you will note that many of them were secured as a direct result of a properly applied "education."

It should be manifestly clear to you now that we are operating in a very special place in Our Father Below's lowerarchy of needs and why we are not seeking to "destroy" Sardis Christian. Our success here will greatly increase the effectiveness of our tempters across the board by leaving the Enemy's people under-equipped for the battles they will face. Further, we will play a key role in the undoing of many a poor sot's faith while securing for Our Father some of his best future operatives. With the progress already made in the western education systems, we will do so almost at our ease.

I advise you, therefore, to embrace our calling—my calling. Of course, if you would prefer, I could have you transferred to the East, perhaps to the Chinese theater? There it costs the little pigs something real to follow the Enemy instead of just a bit of disapproval from peers. I've seen those saints, and they are terrible.

Yours Infernally,

Wrackturn

-3-
Whose University is It?

My Dear Nobshank,

We should now return to the question of overall strategy. We must anticipate how to "guide" the school into our fold, how to "bend" it into view with Our Father Below's dark-hearted, all-encompassing will. For this, we cannot take account of only this generation or of even the next; we must play the long game. The first and most obvious question is this: Exactly whose university is this going to be?

Now, of course they're always giving lip service to the idea that it "belongs" to the Enemy, but that doesn't really answer our question. The Enemy allows them to exercise all manner of free will, and He does not specifically compel them in any given direction at all times. That means that while the school as a whole might be "dedicated" to the Enemy, it is actually *controlled* and *run* by real, live, breathing individuals—individuals who are not predestined always to make the right decisions. It is the Enemy's great folly, and we have used it to our advantage time and again. The organization will "belong" at any and all given times to a particular person or small group and they can choose to follow the Enemy or to listen to us. It is a very heavy burden to carry. After all, if that Paul fellow reasonably warns against becoming a teacher, imagine being responsible for a whole gaggle of them! So, our challenge is to identify that person or group who will wield real power and to attach ourselves to them early. In the private Christian university system, these schools trend toward taking one of two main routes forward: a genuine, potent board of trustees or a practical family dynasty.

Allowing the former is a risky proposition and if it happens, we will have to act proactively and exercise significant subtlety. If H. James considers giving up control in a system where real power is held by the school's board, it is a sign that he is taking his role as custodian for the Enemy very seriously. He realizes that this isn't *his* school. Worse, he understands his own limitations and is seeking out others to hold himself accountable. It is a very dangerous situation. If it succeeds, the university will be self-propagating in its mission and authority will be spread around via a system of checks and balances. In that case, the board will, in theory, look for the best qualified, most spiritually sincere candidate for the chancellorship when necessary. We will have no clear way of knowing whom they might consider, and so advance preparation of the next generation of administration isn't possible. This leaves us scrambling with each new appointment to re-establish control of the school in order to maintain a firm grip.

But if that sounds all too bad, be patient. There are opportunities! We may not be able to predict who will be considered for the chancellorship beforehand, but by the successful corruption of the board itself, we can control the choice when it comes. It is therefore possible to steer the board toward our preferred candidates, or at least away from the ones we thoroughly dislike. We also can entrench ourselves in the levels of bureaucracy below the chancellor, starting with the provost. When a new appointment is made, even in the worst-case scenario, where a sincere believer manages to slip through our lines and into the chancellorship, he or she will be met on all sides with anger, frustration, and resistance.

Perhaps most advantageous, though, is that if we manage to create the proper balance, the ultimate location of our power remains almost completely anonymous. You may be surprised to hear that the vast majority of students at these schools don't even know what a board of trustees is or what it does, let alone who any of them are. The faculty knows more, but not one in a dozen has ever even met a member of the board, let alone knows any of them well enough to actually communicate with them about anything of significance. This allows us to comfortably isolate the board members and hide our activities by making certain they are only exposed to certain points of view. Better, the board itself fades into the background. If someone begins to get an inkling of us, they almost always focus their attention on the chancellor or provost, who we can then replace, giving the critics an empty victory while we simply bring in our next tool. All in all, it can be an admirable system created out of what could be a very bad situation for us.

As luck would have it, though, I believe Sardis will most likely take another path. These evangelical schools have a tendency to keep it "all in the family," as it were, and therein lies our second strategic option. For one reason or another, they have resisted the temptation to set up their ministries as independent operations. Instead, they run them like a family business, the fathers grooming the sons to take over leadership when they are gone. While some of the meatbags tend to associate this approach with one family or another, in truth there is a whole raft of them floating down the river: Trinity Northern, Freedom Baptist, Faith Evangel, Philadelphia, George Armstrong, and of course Sardis Christian are a non-inclusive list. They all share one point in common: They were begun by a single visionary leader and that leader or his family maintains tight control of the university administration.

You can see why this seems like an attractive option. As you well know from your historical studies at the TTU [Tempter's Training University], we have successfully employed a "divide and conquer" strategy of secularization at most of the previous generation of schools. One response to it is for the founder who created the original vision to maintain an iron grip on things. If he sees the school begin to deviate from the Enemy's path, he can then right his own ship. Of course, he cannot live forever, so he must pass that responsibility on to someone else. Who can he trust more fully than his own flesh and blood, someone who has been carefully groomed for such "a high and lonely destiny"?

You can also see, I expect, why this is such an advantageous path for us. Yes, it is true that a "benevolent dictator" can stand in our way. Fortunately for us, centralizing power in that same dictator is the chink in their armor. Any person powerful enough to thwart our plans is also sufficiently strong enough to enforce them. We have simply to "enlighten" that one person or that one family and the rest of the university will fall into line. Afterward, when the Perception of Inherited Belief comes into play, our triumph is virtually assured. What this strategy lacks in subtlety and finesse, it more than makes up for in brutal effectiveness when properly deployed.

Globnobber informs me that he has already effectively seeded this idea in Newritch, Sr.'s head and he seems to be taken in. His thought is already overcome with fear of our accomplishments at other schools and his personality is such that he has trouble trusting others to do jobs he considers of the utmost importance. To that end, he has taken steps to neuter the board of trustees and to pack it with members personally loyal to him and to his family. Attach yourself to his oldest child, Elderson Newritch, whom we can presume will be the heir apparent. Make him your particular subject of specialization. From here on, we want to encourage all involved to treat SCU as if it were one of the old duchies or kingdoms, to be reflexively passed down through the family. Elderson should see it as his father's personal property—that is enough for now.

We shall see how this develops. For the time being, be ready to pivot back to the earlier strategy if needed. Get to know Elderson. Get to know him well and let me know your insights.

Yours Infernally,

Wrackturn

-4-
Hubris & Success

My Dear Nobshank,

Very good. I see from your enthusiastic reaction that you are coming along swimmingly and have a much better grasp of our task and its possible benefits. And, yes, there is an incredibly delicious irony in creating a school that, while acting in the hated name of the Enemy, in fact abuses/corrupts some of His most powerful saints, subverts the faith of His children, and seriously damages the credibility of His church in the eyes of the very mission field it claims to be trying to reach! I am of the firm belief that it will result in perhaps the most delicious vintage of souls since the corrupted Puritan. But once again, let us not get ahead of ourselves. The deed still must be accomplished, and we have some idiotically sincere faith to manage and manipulate. How should we bypass the defenses Sardis Christian University has erected against us? In terms of overarching theme, the answer is simple: hubris and success.

"Surely," you may be thinking, "he meant to write 'success and hubris.'" After all, according to conventional wisdom, success is what breeds hubris, and therefore, I am putting the effect before the cause. To that, I say that we are not bound by the limited vision of lesser tempters.

The reason for this is demonstrated in your somewhat mediocre description of the administration's philosophy of faculty interaction. You are correct that they reserve the right to terminate a faculty member's employment each year without warning or excuse, a process referred to on the ground as "nonrenewal" (which to them somehow sounds less offensive than "firing" or even "letting go"). This, of course, is increasingly becoming the norm in higher education as a whole, as we encourage the delightful practice of adjunct abuse. At several of these "Christian" schools, however, it takes on a certain "flavor," as it is justified and even taken as a point of pride. Note that while this may seem on the surface to be a reasonable defense against leftward drift, it isn't actually aimed at anything in particular, at least not in the policy itself. Yes, it can be used to prevent the introduction of heresy, but it can also be used to get rid of any faculty member for any reason whatsoever. In fact, no reason is needed other than an "I don't like you" from the right person in the right place inside the administration. This is not accidental, and it should be left particularly vague at Sardis.

The not-so-subtle undercurrent here is obvious. Exercising complete and total control over another person's livelihood, especially when that person has a family, is a form of power at its most raw. It infects all interactions between the two parties. Even if there were, in the beginning, some modicum of trust between them, the creation of this dynamic destroys it. None but the most daring (or foolish) will speak their minds on anything but the most inane topics for fear they will in fact be cutting their own throats. Further, since there is no built-in check on the administration's power here, no precedent of future trust can be set. Even if a faculty member is "graciously" allowed to speak his or her mind now, that is no guarantee that the next time won't be a bridge too far.

To hold this level of power over another person with no limit is nothing but naked hubris. No reasonable person would object to placing some restrictions on faculty opinion and action given the historical reality of our successes at other schools and the invention of MeTube, but arrogance of this kind can easily be pushed beyond reason. The fact that the administration leaves no room for the faculty to hold *it* accountable implies that it does not feel the need to be held accountable. It is above such things. And, if accountability were to be needed, it certainly wouldn't come from an inferior bunch such as the faculty.

We can see the absurdity of it with crystal clarity. Sardis specifically reaches out to and hires a whole cadre of (from the Enemy's perspective) intelligent, dedicated, educated believers, some of whom are far more advanced in the Enemy's service than the average person, and all of whom have some strength that the school lacks. The administration places these people in positions of authority over dozens of other fellow believers specifically because they want them to pass along their intelligence, dedication, education, and spiritual maturity. Then the administration threatens them with effectual disbarment and their families with hunger and discomfort if they speak their minds! This level of spiritual turbidity beggars the imagination. Yes, Nobshank. They will actually do all that and more. It is a delicious reality for us.

If you play your hand carefully, then, one of their main defenses becomes ours. You need not fear it in the least. Walk right by it, in fact. While they may perhaps claim a few casualties here and there amongst your tempters' subjects attempting to infiltrate the faculty, they will not touch those you will be placing amongst the administration itself. They are not looking for you there. They do not feel they need to be.

Thus, we will upset the order of things a bit and begin our assault relying upon your Subject's hubris first instead of his success. I know Globnobber has been working this angle for some time with good results. From there, the success, when it comes, will have a most satisfactory reinforcing effect upon your Subject's views. It should create a most effective smokescreen for our infiltration.

Keep me abreast of developments.

Yours Infernally,

Wrackturn

-5-
Corrupting the Core

My Dear Nobshank,

I see from your suggestions about your Subject's growing interest in political engagement that you still have a lot to learn on the issue. Let me share with you some insight I learned manipulating one of my more recent (and best behaved) patients, currently headquartered at 235 Cannon Hob, Washington: Politics, in itself, is neither helpful nor harmful to our cause. It all lies in how we convince our target to place it in relation to the Enemy and His directives.

At the core of his or her being, each of the little beasts has something called a "self-image," and grasping this concept is key in knowing how best to leverage your situation. This "self-image" is, in effect, what they believe themselves to be, often erroneously. In a real way, it controls everything the brutes do, and it influences every decision they make.

I understand that this is a concept completely alien to your mind, but you must simply take it as granted. As they are not gifted with the privilege of living as pure spirit, their eyes cannot see the glaring and painful luminescence of the Enemy that reveals all things as they truly are. By that light, which, to paraphrase the provost-chancellor emeritus, "forms a background of permanent pain to our existence," we see our cruelties, our successes, our failures, and our ultimate futures with perfect clarity. They "see through a glass darkly" and so are constantly guessing at what is on the other side.

At the center of this murky core is a definition of themselves that they consider to be the most essential. It is their Prime, their First Cause. They then build up their larger image structure on this foundation. As with any engineering project, the final result is greatly influenced and even controlled by what they choose to lay down first. Once an intelligent tempter has convinced his subject to adopt a suitable foundation, the rest becomes easy. For example, if you convince them to see themselves first and foremost as a martyr, then everything else that happens to them in their lives will become a further proof of their martyrdom, even things that are entirely their own fault.

But what has this to do with politics? Isn't this all sophomore-level psychology from Temptation 201? It has everything to do with it. Let me give you a more specific example from the subject mentioned above at Cannon Hob.

This particular subject is a man. What's more, he claims very loudly to be from that faction of the Enemy's camp they call "Catholic." He is also very proud to call himself a "Liberal." (This is a somewhat tortured word that can mean he has a serious concern for his fellow humans but, in the particular context of those who think like this subject, refers to a person who makes their political decisions as an effective atheist. They pay little to no attention to the Enemy or His Book, believing both to be quaint, self-reporting personal affectations, somewhat like a preferred flavor of ice cream or a favorite time of year). Now, in his self-image, I was able to convince him to adopt "Liberal" as his center starting point, with his "Christianity" built up from it. The key here is that it is his identity as a liberal that controls his view of his Catholicism, not vice versa. And the results are better than I could have hoped. As hard as it might be to believe, this man actively sponsors and promotes the genocide of an entire class of human beings—children, no less—and still considers himself to be a "good Christian." In fact, he regularly promotes our very own line of moral reasoning to an entire country, helping to ensure that we will have ever more pain and suffering to enfold in our larders. With the added fermentation of so much moral guilt mixed in and well-marinated, I can tell you that his soul will be a sweet morsel indeed when we have finally milked it dry! And it will all be made possible by this conception of himself as a Christian Liberal instead of a Liberal Christian.

Now, it is well known in all quarters of Hell that H. James Newritch is very active in his nation's politics. That is one reason why he founded his school; he hopes to invade all fields of the culture war with the putrid Gospel of the Enemy, especially politics. You are right to suspect that this in itself is a dangerous idea. We've worked hard to transform the idea of separation of the church from the state into that of the exclusion of the church by the state. The idea of a fully integrated faith that seeks to treat everyone with love and charity, even in the political sphere, is one that must be stamped out immediately! Fortunately, with a little leading, I believe you can set your Subject on the right path and therefore eliminate any lasting potential threat his father might have posed.

Use the strategy I outlined above. You must begin to convince your Subject that he is a Conservative who happens to also be a Christian, and not at all a Christian with conservative views. H. James himself often seems to be confused on this point, thanks in no small part to Globnobber's expert ministrations. That has no doubt created a state of confusion in the mind of your own Subject from an early age. Further, prod him to see "conservative" and "Christian" not as complementary terms, but as actual synonyms. If a thing is "conservative" it must be "Christian", and if a thing fits his definition of "Christian" it must be "conservative." If successful, before many more years pass you'll have him betraying both movements when the whim suits him, all with the approval of his own conscience.

And do not let the seeming conflict between "conservative" and "liberal" delay or discombobulate you. The Enemy is only interested in either insofar as they line up with the views expressed in His Abhorrent Book. The particular historical manifestations of both waffle back and forth on that point, each one sometimes closer to His standard than the other. So, if you can convince your Subject to adopt any standard instead of the Enemy's, you have gone a long way toward controlling his actions and sealing his fate.

Ironically, each brute can usually see a clearer picture of the truth about the others than they can see of themselves. Once you have succeeded in placing Our Father Below's preferred ideas in your Subject's center, your main task will be to prevent others from revealing the truth about him to himself. Thankfully, though, that is usually an easy task. Nothing scares these meatbags as much as the possibility of finding out what others *really* think about them.

Yours Infernally,

Wrackturn

-6-
Measuring Success

My Dear Nobshank,

In one of my letters, I mentioned we would be launching our initial assault via hubris first as an advance strike and then reinforcing it with several waves of success. I want now to outline a foundation for a kind of success that will have nothing to do with the Enemy and everything to do with us. No single letter would be sufficient to explain such a broad topic; therefore it shall be a continuing area of correspondence and research. Let us deal first with the general idea of success and how the school should measure it.

Success is a very important staple of human existence. Whether in the Enemy's camp or not, they seem to be born with an innate need to experience it, and they often measure their entire life's worth by the amount of it they've accumulated. That is very curious, given that most of them haven't the foggiest idea what they mean by the word and don't know what to do with success once they have it. It is much like a drug for many of them. The more they have of it, the less it satisfies them, and the worse they want more of it. As often as not, it becomes all-consuming and can be a means to destroy them. At its most basic, success is simply the realization that a particular intentional cause or causes has, in fact, resulted in a specific desired effect or effects. Therefore, success in itself and by itself is indicative of nothing other than to show that something happened and something else followed it. Obviously, in the abstract, no specific cause or effect is good or bad. It all depends on whether the process accomplishes the Enemy's Will or that of Our Father Below.

That of course won't prevent the meatbags from making much more out of various successes and failures than is warranted. It is a shortcoming almost universal in their species: as they are attuned to our world but cannot see it directly, they tend to look for meaning in everything, even when it isn't there. Frequently, they blindly take any success at all as proof of the Enemy's blessing and their own superior worth when very often the facts indicate neither.

Your job is to encourage your Subject to measure the success or failure of SCU entirely by our terms. "Is the campus getting bigger? Is the student body growing? Are the students enjoying themselves? Can students easily borrow money? Have we secured only the biggest names in media, music, and politics for our chapel services? Are we making money hand over fist?" Those are the kinds of questions you want him asking. I think you'll find it very easy to focus his mind on these points.

At the same time, you will want to steer his mind away from gauging his school's success by the intangible, spiritual measures by which the Enemy will gauge him in the long run of eternity. "Are the students becoming more like Him (the Enemy)? Are the professors holding students to the highest academic standards? Are students graduating debt-free, ready to enter the field of ministry? Is the school remaining focused on its mission? Are our resources and improvements supporting our mission? Am I leading the institution well by example? Do people trust me more than they fear me? Am I myself working hard to become the kind of person I know He (the Enemy) wants our students to become?" The moment you see his mind starting to drift toward one of these, quick action is necessary or you may lose your Subject, not to mention the university!

In this task, you're aided by the fact that there is nothing inherently wrong with anything in the first set of questions. The fact is that if his school is going to function well, it does need money. If the school is going to effectively serve its students, it must continue a series of capital improvements to its buildings and campus. The Enemy does want the students to enjoy themselves, and He has no particular objection to everyone being paid nicely for a job well done. Massage his conscience with the knowledge that these are all good things that the Enemy does want him to think about, just in a subtly different order. Twist it all around and distract him from thinking of the larger picture. Make what should be the side effects of seeking the Enemy earnestly become instead ends in themselves, and gradually elevate them until, without realizing it, he will come to idolize them over and above the Enemy Himself.

With the proper preparation, he'll never notice what we are about until you meet him at the very end. I know the wait will be a difficult one, but you can look forward to the shock in his eyes, and until then, we will have a steady stream of his students upon which to feast.

Yours Infernally,

Wrackturn

-7-
Servants & Customers

My Dear Nobshank,

From what you reported in your last letter, I am quite pleased with your progress. The university is increasingly focused first and foremost on improving its public standing and its physical circumstances. It has not yet come to neglect its spiritual calling, but give it time. Our goal is to first give them that taste of our brand of success, and then gradually to wean them off the Enemy's. All in good time. Let us now take the next steps to make that happen. Sardis Christian University needs customers.

As a reminder, you want to continue to encourage all school leadership to regard all success, especially monetary, as "proof" that the Enemy is pleased with them. It should never occur to them to question the means or the mode of any particular success. If someone does, he or she may well discover us. Still, I believe the chances of that are small. The general faith in H. James and his mission is strong and they will be slow to examine anything received from him, such as the goal of building this university bigger than the nearby University of Ohio at all costs. More likely, they will see any progress toward that vision as good by definition, however it may be achieved. Further, for all the lip service they give the Enemy's warning that Our Father Below prowls about the earth like a roaring lion, they rarely live like it. Their thinking is profoundly simplistic: if the thing I am doing is getting bigger and

24

becoming easier, the success must be from God. If what I am doing is struggling or getting more difficult, the problems must be of the Devil. The idea that any particular instance could be one, the other, or neither rarely enters into their calculations. Your Subject and his school should be no different.

Now, our next step is a small one, but it will net some very satisfactory results. H. James Newritch came to prominence in a time when we had used socialism and communism to great effect. He jumped on board the great American ideological crusade against both, and as a result, his university has been pushing capitalism as a response. Rather than unnerve Our Father Below, this was a most welcome development. In the face of a real threat, the American conservative church was easily convinced not simply to appreciate capitalism, but to worship it. Skillful management has led many of them to adopt capitalism as a form of replacement Christianity. (This is a happy byproduct of seeing themselves as conservatives first and Christians second.) We now get down to some brass tacks of this wonderful combination.

As you know, the Enemy has the most unnatural and disgusting ideas about morality, especially when compared with the endless practicality of Our Father Below. While I could speak at length and in great detail of all the ways this is so, I wish to draw your attention to His laughable idea that it is better to be a servant than a lord. In His ridiculous economy, He would rather see the meatbags seeking to serve and love each other than to control and dominate. You would think, therefore, that creating servant-leaders would be a central element of anything Sardis Christian University does. If the Enemy were to have His way, it would be. We have other ideas.

Your immediate plan should be to coordinate with Globnobber and introduce to the university administration the "radical" idea that they are "doing it all wrong." Show them the past abuses of western education, with its (very real) domination of students by arrogant faculty; you can use the phrase "Sage on the Stage" to great effect here. Suggest to them the parallels between this kind of education and the socialistic tyrannies they love to hate so much. A capitalistic response should immediately suggest itself. When it does, shove it as far to the right side of the spectrum as possible.

In particular, you want to spark an "innovation" (they love that word) and alter the relationship between the administration and the students. They should begin to think of and treat students as customers instead of actual pupils or Christian believers. This shift will seem subtle at first, but its results will be ultimately dramatic. Servants care more about other people than they do for themselves. Servants seek to do honor to someone else. Servants are humble in demeanor and dedicated to their Master, the Enemy. Customers, on the other hand, are none of those things. Customers are focused on getting what they want. Customers are arrogant, demanding, and manipulative. Best of all, "the customer is always right." A student who is "always right" is no student at all. Such a person has nothing to learn and will gain nothing from an education. Therefore, in just this one shift, we will have undone virtually everything the Enemy hopes to accomplish with SCU. (But do not worry—I have no intention of stopping there.)

For our more immediate purposes of manipulating the impression of success, once this change is fully realized, the best of results should quickly follow: a most satisfactory and dramatic rise in enrollment. This should not be surprising and is not indicative of anything other than a law of human nature. Specifically, when you give the meatbags what they want, they will flock to you and throw their money at you. It is as true of pornography and professional sports as it is with "Christian" education, and hence it will enhance the university's sense of "success" (entirely on our terms). On the contrary, it is to be hoped that the Enemy will be profoundly displeased by all this and will one day move to judge it. But not too soon. Given His disturbing patience with the creatures, it is to be hoped that we can milk the situation for some time before He decides to move. Anticipating your question about the faculty, I wouldn't worry about them. First, we have made some further progress in taking away the few prerogatives they still enjoyed. Second, if you change the relationship between the administration and the students, you will change the faculty by default, and in most pleasing ways. If students are customers and the administration the senior management, that makes the faculty into customer service representatives. They can be abused, appealed over, ignored, disrespected, etc., in just the same way someone might a…(What are they called? Ah! yes!)…telemarketer. Even better, the students themselves will become almost a sort of secret police—always watching and reporting on things they dislike or disapprove of. That should reduce honest interactions and mentorships very nicely. The faculty who recognize this and oppose us can be easily written off as entitled whiners who aren't *really* interested in the good of the students so much as they are the loss of unearned prestige—as indeed will be true of more than a few.

Don't worry about the trustees either. With our successful appointments there, I doubt a less useful group could be conceived…unless you happen to need a rubber stamp.

Yours Infernally,

Wrackturn

P.S. Speaking of telemarketers—have you heard that they are now considering opening a further circle of Hell, just for them? To date they've been sent to the "Special Hell" reserved for people who talk at the theater, but apparently Our Father Below does not feel they are buried deeply enough. I myself would prefer to see them consolidated with the spammers.

-8-
Curriculum Adjustments

My Dear Nobshank,

I can see from your inclusion of the faculty senate minutes that the administration has presented our proposal for an "Office of Student Satisfaction @ Sardis Christian University." The faculty winced and a few were outraged, but no one seriously opposed the move. Remember, you are aiming to take this farther than just providing students with a feeling of fulfillment over a job well done. The school's whole purpose should revolve around giving students what they *want* as opposed to what they *need*. This office presents your chance to set up an adversarial relationship between customer-students and faculty. This also means that we can begin our next step: Curricular Adjustments.

I suppose it is high time to discuss study and how we want them to do it. For this, I really must harken back to and adapt the advice given by another fine tempter: We don't usually force our subjects to read this or that book, listen to this or that podcast. The trick is, really, to get them to habitually avoid exposing themselves to certain ideas. If you can succeed there, it will be only a matter of time before they fill their heads with nonsense on their own. In the end, it really doesn't matter what kind they put in as long as what is coming out is what we want.

Now, I don't intend to get into too many prescriptive details here. You know very well the kinds of books, websites, lectures, etc., they should avoid and there are any number of lists available on the infernet. What is special in the case of Sardis Christian University is we will be using the students themselves to purge objectionable material from the curriculum. Now that the university has begun to be customer-focused, all we need to do is convince the customers what kind of content they want and then they will use the administration to bring the faculty to heel. Enough whining on the course surveys and the school will self-censure! It will be another sweet irony that their own faculty committees will be forced to make the changes. Here are some ideas you can coordinate with the SCU Tempters Assembly:

- Remind them, and the administration, of the real purpose of an education, which is to get a degree that will supposedly guarantee the "right" to earn a certain amount of money: The thought that education is about building themselves into better, stronger people who are more like the Enemy should never enter their thoughts.

- Train them to think entirely in terms of entertainment: This is a larger process we've been working on with the current generation, but you should encourage it. Curriculum and classes are either "fun" or they are "too hard" and "unfair." Let there be nothing in between.

- Make them comfortable: Customers do not like being pushed beyond their comfort zone. Convince them any ideas or sources that contain material that could in any way challenge them is somehow unfair and discriminatory.

- Keep them focused on *popular* books and sources: If the book or lecture isn't by some famous person, it isn't worth their time. Popular sources aimed at the lowest common denominator promote the blandest possible content while creating the illusion of depth and profundity. They make readers *believe* they are being deep when in reality they are not.

- Inculcate a disdain for old books: The idea here is to lead them to believe that if something is newer, it must represent "progress" and is therefore better. Alternatively, if the students are a lazy bunch, pointing out that older books are harder to read and understand can work. In any event, creating an artificial focus on "new" and "popular" sources will close them off from the aid of *thousands* of the Enemy's greatest warriors.

- Encourage them to judge books by their covers: And not just their covers. They should also be quick to judge and reject anything without pictures. When they complain, you can prod the professors to ask, "Would you like crayons with that?"—which is an effective way to build up resentment.

- If all else fails, encourage them to study quickly and not deeply: In keeping with the goal of completing their degree, if they must read and study, you want them to plow through it as quickly as possible and with little to no time given to actual consideration of what they're studying. You can distract them with relationships, games, outdoor adventures, whatever. The distractions themselves need not be evil at all.

Of course, it may be that you will still encounter some resistance from various quarters of the faculty senate, but they should be easily managed. The techniques for dealing with professors are old and well established. Play off their usually inflated sense of accomplishment and superiority. These are people who have worked very hard to gain admission to the ranks of an exclusive club. Those who have PhDs will be tempted to become absurdly sure of themselves; those who do not have them will be insecure and defensive. In all cases, they were hired because they were "experts." Exploit that. When the administration (or even other faculty) have critiques for faculty-initiated proposals in the senate, have tempters propose that those suggestions—any suggestions, really—are a personal affront to the faculty member's professionalism and prerogative in the classroom. When the critiques are too good to be ignored, first have faculty blow up out of "principle" and then, after changes are made, irritate the fancied wound and make it impossible to forget. I have some pet professors I have worked with who are still muttering in Hell about academic disagreements from a century ago.

In the senate as a whole, of course, you can play up these sentiments in any number of ways, but I would have your tempters focus specifically on wordsmithing the proposals as they come out from the committee. Everyone in the room knows already that they have no actual say in the matter and that the senate at SCU has no real power. If the administration wants a proposal passed, it must be, else the nonrenewals will be forthcoming. Still, at least some of them feel as if they must do *something*. Dickering over the precise placement of every "and," "but," "or," "the" gives them something useful to do. Useful to your purposes, of course. For the wordsmiths, the whole process feels empty and a little humiliating. For everyone else, there is nothing quite so irksome as spending an hour of precious time accomplishing nothing at all.

When it all comes down to it, that is what this is about—nothing. Or, if we are successful, it shall be.

Yours Infernally,

Wrackturn

-9-
The Perception of Inherited Belief

My Dear Nobshank,

You continue to demonstrate your...adequacy. My sources tell me that the faculty senate is a morass of frustration and wasted time. Between the administration's paranoid meddling and the senate's obsessive wordsmithing, it takes them six months or more to change a course description. Just take care to make them as cynical about the process as possible. The Enemy will still honor even pointless work if it is done with a cheerful heart.

Your news that the Old Man has decided to retire, and that his health situation is such that he will likely separate himself from day-to-day university business in a real way, is well met indeed. Just as expected, he has appointed your Subject to replace himself. I expect you have already convened your Tempters Assembly! The reason for our haste is that we have a relatively narrow window of opportunity and we must make the most of it if we are to bring about the undoing of what the Old Man spent his life trying to accomplish. It is time to leverage the Perception of Inherited Belief. Many second-rate tempters who have not studied human history closely overlook the PIB, but understood fully, it becomes very useful.

I presume you are familiar with this concept? As we have noted, Nobshank, the humans still exist in that state of imperfection called "free will" and the Enemy does not cajole or force them to live a certain way, even as He predestines their ultimate fates. They are not guided by any single specific will (as we are) and when they try to force their will on others, those others tend to rebel—much as Our Father Below once did.

In fact, it is impossible for any human decision or belief to be passed from one to another under compulsion. They can encourage each other to accept this or that belief. They can seduce or threaten one another. They can even torture and murder each other, but in the end, the only way for a thought to be imputed to any particular person is for that person to decide to take ownership of it. Even then, it is very likely that one or another detail will be lost or misunderstood. Therefore, no matter how well-laid out a vision may be for them, they tend to stray from it.

As a result, it is very difficult for humans to maintain their mission focus for very long. I can understand how this fact isn't intuitive to superior beings like ourselves. We of pure, sublime, and eternal spirit, whose choices have been steeled to perfection in the image of Our Father Below, may alter our immediate goals but our motivations and ultimate ends are set. The idea that we could lose focus on Our Father's will is as alien to us as the idea of living outside of the timestream is to them. But whether we comprehend it or not, this loss of focus is an almost daily reality for the meatbags.

This is especially true when they try to pass a particular mission between more than one generation. The experiences and decisions of the fathers and mothers are not guaranteed to pass on completely (or at all) to the sons and daughters. Further, the transitions are fraught with confusion, fear, suffering, loss, and sadness. Even without our tender ministrations in their time of need (and of our opportunity) it would be a difficult process and undoubtedly some aspects would be lost. Our goal is to encourage the perception that the belief and mission have been proactively maintained, while enforcing a reality that repudiates both. If successful, we will soon have them violating the Enemy's dictums in the Enemy's own name and feeling self-righteous for doing so.

Allow me to illustrate: You can think back to your human studies courses at the TTU, particularly to the American Puritan campaign. Recall what happened as the first generation of Separatists and Puritans began to transition to the second. The original Pilgrims, as they were called, were an incredibly dedicated bunch. They had independently arrived at their disgusting idealistic conclusions and they were determined to stick by them. We threw almost everything we had at them—persecution by the government, discrimination by their peers, fear of death, opportunities for racism, etc. We manipulated the situation so that they had to debark to the "new" world at the worst time of year so that many of them died, tempting the others to despair. We created cultural misunderstandings that, had this been Jamestown, would have resulted in open war with their neighbors. Through it all, their defenses held. They never gave up their faith and they continued to treat their new neighbors with respect. For a time, it looked as if all was lost…

…and then came the PIB. Their children and their grandchildren "inherited" their religion, but not their personal belief in it. More and more people took it piecemeal and with conditions. Some wanted to start making more money in addition to living a Christian life. Others wanted to expand their colony and build a greater settlement. They all wanted the social advantages of church membership without the responsibilities that came with it. With masterful manipulation, the tempters of the time entered through the gaping holes in their spiritual defenses. The result? By the third generation, they were accepting slaves into the colony and embarking on wars of near genocide against their neighbors. All of this, yet to *their* minds they were still as strong in their pursuit of the Enemy as their ancestors had been. Today, Plymouth and Boston represent our crowning achievements on the eastern seaboard of North America. Have you caught the vision? Given that your Subject was born into his father's belief and is now set to inherit a university supposedly dedicated to it, you should have little trouble muddling his mind on these points. Keep him focused with confidence on the idea that he is a Christian because his father was before him and because that is the society in which he moves. Keep him far away from any thought whatsoever about the moment when he chose to stand personally in the Enemy's camp and what that means for his daily life, how he treats people, and the specific moral decisions he makes for his university.

We here aim to divert your Subject from a sincere, personal attempt to follow the original mission of his father and, indeed, the Enemy Himself. Instead, we want to help him erect an idol in his mind—an idol that will be identified with the material prosperity and fame of his personal university. Once that point of view is firmly entrenched, you can expect him to begin associating his wants and his definition of "success" (with which we have supplied him) with the "obvious" will of God. Whole kegs of sweet-scented hypocrisy are sure to follow!

In fact, I am sending along a flask for you to fill for me. While it will be some time before it is aged enough to really improve itself, a small taste right now will give me an idea of where else we might take this in order to produce the best flavors.

Yours Infernally,

Wrackturn

-10-
Taming the Faculty

My Dear Nobshank,

No doubt you will be disappointed to hear that your attempt at informing the Department of Logistics of my harmless request for a pre-taste of your Subject's hypocrisy has been intercepted and dealt with. You forget that I did not supplant my predecessor without cultivating a wide influence. This is for the best, though. For a while I was concerned that you were beginning to show some actual loyalty to me and to the department. That, of course, is unacceptable. Very soon we shall restore some balance and a proper fear to your outlook. You can expect agents from the Office of the Coordinator for the Advancement of Fiendish Excellence to visit you presently for some "professional development."

Speaking of the happy topic of professional development, for this letter, I want to turn back to the university's faculty. As you have discovered, a central point in our campaign is to undermine and corrupt the faculty itself. They are the Enemy's front line in the battle for souls at Sardis Christian University, and while we may enjoy our fun thoroughly corrupting the administration, if the administration does not then corrupt/interfere with the faculty, we have accomplished nothing of lasting value. Thankfully, this largely takes care of itself: most faculties in modern higher education and historically are a morass of bloated egos, wounded pride, and petty jealousies. Still, there is much we can do to take what is naturally bad and make it far worse.

To begin with, you should look to incubate the kind of relationship between the administration and the faculty as mirrors our own best management practices. What you want to create in the faculty is an atmosphere of constant, low-grade fear, rather than trust or respect. They are employees and expendable and should be constantly reminded of that fact. What you want to create in them is an appearance of "loyalty," but a very shallow one that just barely obscures the fear or greed lurking beneath it. The fear is that they may lose their position if they don't do precisely what the leadership wants and the greed whispers that if they will only say what the administration desires to hear, they can advance up the power structure, make more money, become marginally famous, etc. Have your tempters carefully distract the faculty from anything like serious self-examination; all their problems come to them through the administration. And don't bury their fear too deeply. Make sure that objective observers in the administration can see this narcissism and simpering for what it is, and then encourage them to impute that spinelessness to all faculty. Never allow the leadership to ask, "From whence comes the atmosphere in which all this can thrive?" What we want is competition and mutual suspicion, not cooperation and understanding.

The goal is to have both faculty and administration regard each other as stereotypes and as members of an almost tribal organization. "The administration thinks thus and so." "The faculty are like this or that." They will naturally tend to boil that stereotype down to its worst possible common denominators. Then, when they encounter a member of the opposing "tribe," they will automatically assume the worst about that person. In short, they will look at each other and see a myth, not a man or a woman. From that point on, the encounter will become a self-fulfilling prophecy and our job is done. If you are successful, you can create a most unhealthy environment. Each side will build up a permanent animosity toward the other and, eventually, let fly their abuse at the least opportunity. Continue to remind your Subject of his non-academic roots and the family's lack of scholarly *dignitas*. This strategy has the potential to work well with any administrator who has not followed a traditional academic path into leadership. Rub it in, and of their own accord you can tempt them to resent faculty as pampered babies who have done nothing "significant" to merit the exalted status society affords them. (They should never begin to ask what qualifies as "significant," especially in the Enemy's eyes.) Encourage them to make it a mission to "put the faculty in their place" or to "tame" them. With a little more finesse, faculty-baiting can become an enjoyable pastime that massages vulnerable egos and imparts a temporary sense of intellectual superiority. As for the faculty, they should reciprocate the attitude admirably with all the laughable indignation of pompous pride offended. Have as many as possible work to undercut the administration, or at least to complain constantly about anything and everything. They should only be encouraged to discover a backbone in ways and at times that reinforce the cherished stereotype of them as petty, rude, whiny, academic-y brats. Parking spaces or office size, for example, are great places to keep them focused.

Much of your ultimate success will depend directly on the behavior and attitudes of your Subject and his appointed leadership. The faculty will be distracted by the students, but it is the administration's job to pay attention to everything, particularly the faculty. If the administration acts, faculty will react. As the head of the administration, your Subject's tone will become the administration's tone. This isn't something to allow him to consider in any introspective sort of way, of course. Don't let him feel this as a "weight" at all. Suggest to him that they are his employees paid to serve him, not real, vulnerable people in need of an actual leader. That should fan the flames of tension nicely.

Ah! But I nearly forgot, I had promised to speak to "professional development." This is a concept the meatbags have that is modeled on some putrid principle of the Enemy's that they should be continually growing toward Him. Even the non-believers there on earth have picked up on this general theme and believe that people should be constantly improving themselves. If allowed to continue unchecked, it would indeed develop into a most dangerous prospect. Thankfully, there is a very easy remedy that turns "professional development" to our advantage.

The key is guiding them in what they intend to develop and the tools they use to supposedly develop it. Remember the idea of steering the students toward "popular" studies? It is the same here. Centralize professional development into a single office or position accountable directly to the chancellor. Then offer a steady stream of low-intensity, vaguely useful-ish (and above all, boring) training opportunities that are inflicted rather than offered. These should focus on the ideas that are most popular in the secular world around them and not eternal truths. You want a "one-size-fits-all" approach where one or two potentates create training for the entire university. Given that there is a very wide array of topics covered by any university and that the people covering them are already experts in their fields, this should effectively insure that any training offered will be very shallow, created by people who have no real idea what the various specialties involve (How can they? No one can specialize in everything.), and therefore will be of little practical use. I understand that it will be difficult to keep out all of the Enemy's content, but we can make very significant headway using this approach.

It is a lovely principle to be teaching at the faculty constantly, distracting from their real work, and yet doing nothing to really educate them. Better, we'll be furthering our project of making them all resent each other in the process.

Send that flask back with my associates. Expect them to squeeze a little of your own anguish into it.

Yours Infernally,

Wrackturn

-11-
Introducing Online Learning

My Dear Nobshank,

We now return to our theme of "success." There has been a revolution slowly brewing in the world of meatbag education. It offers us a chance to throw Sardis Christian toward the head of the pack, degrade the effectiveness of SCU's degrees, and to make millions of dollars for your Subject at the same time. What devilry is this, you may ask? It is something called "Distance Learning." Essentially, it is the old correspondence course repackaged using the internet.

Now, before we go further you must understand that online education, like any other kind, could be very dangerous to us. In fact, intelligently employed, it could be a very potent weapon in the Enemy's modern arsenal. Consider what might happen if millions of people were to suddenly connect with intelligent teaching from the Enemy's perspective! Why, if we are not careful, it could be a significant step toward His abominable goal of spreading His so-called "gospel" to every person on the planet! That, of course, is why we must act promptly and sow seeds early to prevent what could be a real disaster.

Thankfully, the groundwork for our own success is already there, and at SCU it is virtually assured. The administrative bean counters are certain to discover something about online education:

it can be enormously profitable. With the proper equipment, SCU could offer a limitless number of courses to as many people as they like. With no physical campus, the overhead would be drastically reduced—no students to house and feed, no classrooms to light and heat, no roads to maintain, no grounds to keep, etc. Since there would be no brick-and-mortar classrooms for professors to haunt, they need not hire full-time teachers. They can dole out individual classes to off-site professors who have to provide their own office space, equipment, medical coverage, retirement, etc. When a professor ceases to serve his or her purpose, he/she can be jettisoned, and any pretended moral obligation to the "team" quickly forgotten. For this, they will charge close to full-price tuition, as compared to other schools. It is almost highway robbery.

You see, the disastrous scenario where the unadulterated "gospel" is spread to the ends of the earth is only possible if your Subject and the rest of his administrative cronies exercise the most profound self-control and mission-oriented integrity. From the beginning, they would have to be more concerned with advancing the Enemy's kingdom than they are with becoming rich. Even that miscreant Mother Teresa could surely be tempted to milk such a situation for all it was worth! Luckily, we are not dealing with Teresa here. We have already had some success in muddling the mission of the university in significant ways. Further, since we have largely replaced the Enemy's definition of "success" with our own, this new money-making opportunity will fit in seamlessly.

Of course, there really is nothing wrong with making money. There is nothing inherently wrong with being rich. The Enemy allows both and is even happy to see such things happen...when they are kept in proper perspective to Himself. Here, we will follow the same policy that we did with politics. You will find it very easy, I think, to convince your Subject and the rest of the administration to idolize the pursuit of wealth in itself, making it central to SCU's identity. Everything must constantly be bigger, better, louder, more refined, etc., and in order to achieve any of that, they'll need as much money as they can get. They will then sacrifice things the Enemy values more on a metaphorical pagan altar: loving the Enemy, loving their neighbors, living with honor, making peace, expressing gentleness, exemplifying self-control, etc. You can provide them with a thousand different reasons why these sacrifices are really "good," completely obscuring the fact that what they are now worshiping is Mammon and not the Enemy at all. For example, "If I fire this longtime employee (who has a family) without warning, it is 'for the greater good' because it 'enables us to grow the school more effectively.' After all, it's 'just business,'" when what they really mean is "I can save a little money this way. To Hell with how it will affect this other person's life." (Yes. To Hell with them all! Let the sweet nectar flow!)

What we seek is nothing less than the general degradation and demotion of Western education. In that, you will be part of a much greater movement. You must teach the administration to reflexively reject the idea of education as a process of meaningful and consistent improvement and instead encourage them to regard it simply as a product to be sold off a non-existent shelf. The goal of our new education isn't to actually educate; instead it's to sell tuition hours. As with any product, the only limit to the amount of money you can make is the number of people you can trick into buying it. High standards limit your potential customer base by excluding clients. All you need to do in order to make more and more money is a little compromise here, another there. For example, money from a student with a 400 SAT spends just as well as money from someone who earned 1600. If you have stringent admissions standards, you'll be excluding possible paying customers. The answer? Lower your standards as far as you can— abysmally low, in fact—to allow as many people as possible through. Once they're in the program, your goal should be to keep them there as long as you can. Yes, even if you know they will never graduate. Every class a student takes or retakes is that many more tuition hours sold. Who cares if they wash out with a load of student loans and no degree to show for it? You "shared the gospel with them," even as you burdened them with useless debt that may haunt them for the rest of their lives. See how wonderfully evil that is?

Perhaps even better, in this system, students lose their so-called humanity and instead become what we know them to be: resources to be exploited. Since the administration will be working hard to pamper and please them, many students will not even notice the change. Those who do will likely not care. For us, the results couldn't be more promising. Those students who are left behind or who fail out will be abandoned without regret by a system only interested in their money. Those who manage to stay in it will be slowly transformed from servants into customers and, finally, into those little "Christian" devils I mentioned in an earlier letter. They will wend their entitled way through life, stepping on others, and demanding the road be made clear for them or they will harp to the manager. Not only will it do permanent damage to their souls, but their hypocrisy will push thousands of others away from faith in the Enemy.

Not a bad day's work, I would say. Get to it!

Yours Infernally,

Wrackturn

-12-
Sabbaticals and Business

My Dear Nobshank,

It is good to hear that the distance learning money is now flowing freely into Sardis Christian University's coffers. Don't move too quickly or ask for too many compromises too soon. Some of the Enemy's people are, no doubt, prophesying about the dangers of online education and predicting that it will result in a degradation of quality. If you take this where we want it too swiftly, even a complete dolt will see that to be true. On the other hand, if you hold off for a few semesters or even years and make your moves slowly and deliberately, it will be easy for the administration to convince itself that such predictions are really nothing but more hot air from the faculty, something we've trained administrators to believe is all the faculty has to offer. Once the critics have been dismissed, it will be virtually impossible to get your Subject to see the truth of what we've done, even when it is literally right in front of his face.

But there is other important work to do right now. I have confirmed that the provost—the one who still genuinely cares for faculty and education—has recently learned that he has a severe heart condition that will require surgery and at least a year of recuperation. The time to make our next move to take him off the field has come. The first step that you should take is to have your

Subject and the rest of the administration express their most sincere sorrows at the diagnosis and to promise to do anything they can to help. I would even suggest allowing them to be somewhat genuine. You can then use their legitimate feelings to obscure our deeper plan. In an effort to "help," have your Subject offer the provost a sabbatical to recover.

I know that we've taken care to create in the administration a thorough dislike for sabbaticals and you'll have to work around that. We've trained them to think of sabbaticals as "paid vacations" in which "nothing good for the university happens." By that, of course, we mean that the school would earn much more money if the professors teach five or more classes each semester in which we charge each student several thousand dollars. Therefore, each sabbatical is viewed (and resented) as a loss of close to or over a million dollars of potential income to the university! What is advancing the Enemy's cause or pushing the boundaries of human knowledge to that, eh? This has been a most effective way of completely silencing many otherwise potent voices for the Enemy in their culture and keeping powerful ideas and arguments cooped up inside people's heads. So, we don't want to upset a successful system. We need not worry, however. Suggest to your Subject that his offer is a "great" and "kind concession" in acknowledgment of the man's more than forty years of service. (That will also send a most satisfactory message to any faculty still benighted enough to even think about research. If it takes forty years to earn one sabbatical, why bother?)

A "sabbatical" implies that this is a temporary situation. We want the provost and his friends to think that it is. It will help usher him off the stage that much sooner and with less potential squawking. It is normal in a sabbatical to hire someone to temporarily occupy the position. We don't want or need that, because it is the position itself we wish to destroy. We want to break down the wall that protects academics from the business side and the sheer whim of the chancellor's office. Suggest to your Subject that the thing to do is to name the vice president in charge of business affairs as "Acting" Provost. In that one movement, we will have consolidated absolute power in one person, a person who just happens to be concerned first and foremost with earning as much money as possible. With the consolidation, we will have broken the system and removed all practical checks and balances from the situation. While the VP is shrewd enough to move slowly, the deed will be done. You should be able to coordinate the process that will, over time, reduce Sardis Christian University to what they call a "diploma mill." The degrees it grants will be increasingly worthless because they will be purchased instead of earned, but the administration is unlikely to notice (or to care if they do) as long as you keep the money flowing and the building projects increasing in size and absurdity.

You can allow the VP to quietly drop the "acting" bit with little to no fanfare. When the provost recovers and tries to return, he can be quietly shuffled off to retirement. Perhaps with hindsight, he'll come to see that he got off easy.

Yours Infernally,

Wrackturn

-13-
Kingmaking

My Dear Nobshank,

Now that we have ushered the last remaining academic rascal out of the upper administration, it's time to finish your Subject's transition from chancellor to king (or at least a kind of cheap evangelical knock-off).

When we first began this process, the university was, in theory, all about the Enemy. Your Subject's father was dedicated to returning the church to the Enemy and the nation to its Christian roots. As such, though we did make some headway toward muddling him between building his own kingdom and building the Enemy's, we were never able to fully dislodge his idealism. Your Subject, though, is another matter. He is vulnerable in a way that his father never was for the simple reason that he is *not* his father. He must embrace his own mission, and in that process, we have our chance to divert Sardis permanently. We want him to make the school a memorial to himself and to his family, and not about the Enemy at all.

As your Subject begins to actually spend all of that money we're sending him, make sure that he does it in such a way that it fills up the campus with reminders of the specious fact that he and his family are in practice a kind of nobility. The simple but clear message should be obvious: however they may prattle about equality in Christ and being on the same "team," some people are more equal than others. Add plenty of public perks reserved entirely for them and available to no one else, from the simplest and cheapest items to the most outrageous expenses. For example, the two "chancellor" parking spaces outside his corner office cost only a few dollars in paint to create, but what message do they send? No one would notice one—of course the chancellor needs a place to park—but two? It tells anyone paying attention that your Subject isn't simply an employee of a larger endeavor; he and his family are due special treatment because they are inherently better than everyone else. In this specific case, his *wife* has a privileged space that she did not earn, except by her marriage to the king. That fact will not be lost on the handicapped employees who have to pass her spot from that lower lot to get to work. Neither will it be lost on her!

I should think the higher-end perks are obvious, but remember that you can never have too many. The private jet, the "chancellor's dining room," the "chancellor's suite" at each and every sporting venue (complete with the finest food), cars paid for by the school, a salary at least sixteen times larger than the average professor, etc., etc. While for tax purposes these qualify as "university" facilities, in practice, the royal family has priority. Further, when your Subject "allows" another group to use them, you should encourage a strong self-righteous sense of generosity: "See how well I share *my* things?"

Of course, every king should hold court. Once you have these special places dedicated to his highness, create opportunities for the adoring masses to come show fealty. While I doubt you'll be able to convince a real majority to actually worship him, those who do will be loud enough to make their numbers seem much larger than they actually are. Coordinate with their tempters for this purpose. They should treat his every appearance as if a genuine celebrity had walked into the room. Stage the appearances so that he is the center of attention and, if possible, have him waving down from above on his people—his suite in the stadium is a good place for that. While all of this is occupying his attention, you should also begin to make another more subtle move. It is a well-known fact that kings consider themselves to be "above" the law. The royal family of Sardis "Christian" University should be no different. The Student Life Handbook is now famous for its many disgustingly moral strictures (some serious and some silly) including, but not limited to, requiring modest dress, as well as bans on drinking and smoking, distributing unapproved literature, R-rated movies, roleplaying games, and abortion (punishable by fifty demerits, note, but not expulsion). One trained in the Enemy's revolting idea of "fairness" should expect this to be equally restrictive on everyone connected to the university— students, faculty, staff, and of course its leadership. After all, if it is "their" university shouldn't they live by the same rules they impose on others? Ha! Encourage your Subject to feel that neither he nor his family should be bound by the rules of the "lesser" folk, and that the biggest danger isn't hypocrisy, it is getting caught. Therefore, as long as they can use their money and their influence to keep their own lifestyles "quiet," they can live as they like. And for Hell's sake! Keep him off Instapic and Tweeter!

Of course, the truth will leak out and that is a good thing, as long as we maintain plausible deniability. As word spreads, it will undermine the faith of many people dramatically. Even better, the longer you allow self-righteous hypocrisy to ferment and mature, the more the flavor of his soul will pop when you finally get to taste it. I can tell you it will be worth the wait.

Yours Infernally,

Wrackturn

-14-
Inhuman Resources

My Dear Nobshank,

Now, you should turn your attention to providing SCU with something no good tyranny should ever be without: A proper human resources department. Of all the inventions of the modern era, I must say that this is perhaps the most fun.

First, we have the very concept, as implied in the name: human *resources*. "HR" departments, as abstract concepts, really are positioned on the polar opposite end of the spectrum from the Enemy's ideals. The Enemy thinks of each person as an individual soul, worth enough in the grand scheme of things for His Son to commit the Great Atrocity in order to bring them back into relationship with Himself. To HR, people are resources to be mined and managed as efficiently and cheaply as possible. The very fact that a "Christian" organization has adopted that particular terminology is evidence that it doesn't fully understand either the Enemy's mind on those points...or our own. That is all the better for our purposes.

Of course, just because an organization has adopted this particular nomenclature, it does not follow that they have also adopted the deeper philosophy, so it should be your goal to get them to really swallow it whole. Believe it or not, it is often very easy to accomplish this in the case of Christian "ministries," even those still dedicated to their original missions. You do this by exploiting the mission to obscure the mistreatment of the missionaries.

Consider your own field of Sardis University. For years, it has billed itself as a "student-centric" school, dedicated to building up a new generation of "Christ-lovers." In theory, everything at the school is to be focused on this one and only mission, and the administration singularly devoted to it. The result of such a myopic approach is that the administration looks past the people responsible for "ministering." In the administration's mind, faculty and staff have no independent existence apart from their purpose. They are simply tools to be used. That is why one of the most terrifying questions any common-sense person can encounter when applying for work from a supposedly Christian institution is "Will you consider your work here to be a ministry?" That is Christianese for "If you work here, we'll treat you poorly, take you for granted, and lay out unreasonable expectations, but if you complain, you'll be labeled unspiritual and fired."

I suppose you see where this is going? Already, with no specific effort from you or me, the ministries are not aware of their employees as people at all, seeing only the people to whom they minister. Further, since these "means" are working toward a supposedly spiritual "end," the ministries don't so much as pretend such people are due even basic, polite consideration. They are expected to give everything to the mission. If they don't, that is a sign there is something wrong with *them*, not the ministry's leaders. Employees certainly aren't to be treated along anything like the lines laid out in the Enemy's putrid "Golden Rule."

I believe, however, that we can go much further with this at SCU. First, continue to play up the school's status as a *business*. What you want is to breed a kind of dualistic, compartmentalized thinking that keeps their Christianity in one place and their business matters in another, more fundamental one. You will find that you can convince your Subject to justify virtually any sin because it is "just business." In fact, very little makes the meatbags drop their moral compass faster than the excuse that doing so was business-related and "nothing personal." You can think back to our discussion of politics and faith: convince them that they are a business first and a ministry second. Do that, and you've won the battle.

That will dovetail nicely back into HR. The people who work for SCU are tools to be used up and discarded for something new when there is nothing left in them. With a little intelligent manipulation, you can make sure they aren't used well or even intelligently. A good worker, after all, cares for his or her tools. He or she treats them with respect and appreciation. We certainly don't want that! People at SCU should be pushed as hard as possible on the logic that they will one day quit or move on, so the school must get as much out of them as they can while they're there. Attempts to rest after hard work or even to enjoy the simple things in life while toiling onward should be met with scorn or jealousy, taken as proof of laziness. Above all, no one should feel secure or settled. The whole place should be in a constant state of upheaval, from the grounds crew all the way up to the provost. Offices should be dismantled and moved at least once every two to three years, contracts should never come out on time, and everyone should be reminded at least once a semester that there are hundreds of people waiting for his or her job.

All of that should culminate in a stress-filled, dizzying, symphonic cacophony of angst and frustration, with HR providing the very slow dirge-like percussion. Have your tempters assemble regularly report to you on their subjects' blood pressure. If you find they all have prescriptions for diuretics, ACE inhibitors, and medications of that sort, you'll know you're on the right track.

Yours Infernally,

Wrackturn

P.S. Consider moving as many people as possible, particularly professors, into cubicles. Cubicles are a wonderful invention of our logistics department. Nothing tells employees how underappreciated and temporary they are than to be stuck in a cubicle!

-15-
The Personal and the Professional

My Dear Nobshank,

Now that we have established the usefulness of "human resources" in the abstract, I want to continue to make it a bit more practical. While I will be using faculty as my main example, note that this really applies to a broad range of people and positions, each one with its own unique potential to disrupt university spiritual life. Your goal is to break down men and women and to create, in their place, effectual cogs with virtually no outside identity and as few independent thoughts as possible. The tone will be set by your Subject's "leadership" from the chancellor's office, and it will definitely be maintained by his permission. While lesser tempters can get lost in the deceptively complex details, your goal is really quite simple: SCU must slowly and thoroughly break down any barriers between the personal and the professional. In the end, I think you'll agree with the old saying I have on a plaque here in my office that "Hell on earth is birthed in human resources!"

I said "slowly," but really what we want is a full-scale invasion of each employee's personal life, and the sooner you can accomplish that, the better. What we're looking for is the managerial equivalent of our idea of what they call "separation of church and state." In the political realm, you should recall, we have reimagined that separation as wholly one-sided and entirely to our benefit. While its originators intended it to protect the church from meddling by the state, we hope one day to use it to effectively exclude all religious believers from the political decision-making process. Therefore, the secular state is free to legislate to the church at will, while the church is free only to do what the state says. That is precisely the same dynamic we want to create at SCU between the administration and its employees. The school should be free to make whatever demands of the faculty and staff that it wants, and the faculty and staff should feel free to obey those demands without question...or face nonrenewal.

You will find that your efforts will be greatly aided if you work to disseminate two illusions among the faculty and staff. The first is the illusion of ministry and the second is that of loyalty. We've discussed the idea of "ministry" before. Remember, while your Subject thinks of SCU primarily as a business, the image he projects to the larger world is one of a dedicated ministry. Therefore, while he will feel no particular loyalty to his people, he will expect his people to show sacrificial loyalty to himself and to SCU because he is the "general" of a holy army. Encourage him to cut people off immediately and completely if it will save him a dollar and have him reserve the right to place demands on their time without regard for fairness or their family. Good soldiers fighting for the cause should be prepared to sacrifice, after all. If successful, he (and the administration as a whole) will be involved in double-standard decision-making. Any choices they themselves make are "just business" but they will expect everyone else to react to them as if they are a "sacrifice for the mission." If people disagree, well then isn't that just proof that the complainers are really just "Pharisees" unworthy of employment?

Note the one-sided assumption of complete and personal loyalty in this, and you'll want to inculcate it early, because as we progressively undermine the witness of the administration, appeals to ministry will be less and less effective. The secular principle, however, is the same. The administration should feel justified in making any decision they like regarding the life of their people on the grounds that it is "just business" while at the same time expecting absolute and complete loyalty in return—because "it's all about the mission." They should talk a lot about "service" and "team building," but in practice all that should be nonsense. Even the most faithful and long-serving employees should be thrown on the rubbish heap as flagrantly as possible. Then have your tempters ready to exploit that sweet moment when their own subjects finally realize they've been had!

So, what should this look like in terms of day-to-day management? You want your Subject to see to it that SCU infiltrates and finally controls every possible aspect of an employee's life. It isn't enough for the faculty or staff member to give their 40 hours a week. Oh, no. Hell forbid! We want all 168. For residential faculty, they should wake in the morning before dawn to the notifications on their phones, announcing the arrival of new emails. They should teach double the load of most other schools, with expected research requirements on top which they have no hope of realizing. The afternoons should be filled with committee work and the evenings with grading and more email. When summer comes, add in unofficially required load and online course developments (these should not be paid, if at all possible; call them "university service"). Administrators should be sending "Respond Now!" emails and texts at all hours of the day and night. This will exhaust both faculty and the leadership.

Don't neglect to turn the burden of constantly staying in *compliance* into the proverbial vicious cycle in regard to faculty employment. You overwork them and in doing so prevent them from accomplishing research and publication. With no publications forthcoming, they are no longer competitive for new jobs at other schools in the larger academic world. This, in turn, locks them into Sardis as virtually the only place they can find employment, which allows administrators to overwork them further, which puts them farther behind the publication curve, making them more desperate and more subservient as a result. Round and round it goes! If it helps, think of it as a variant of the "sharecropping" system we employed so effectively in the American theater in the aftermath of their little Civil War. Then, we tied African-Americans to their former masters' land by forcing them into greater and deeper debt, leaving them unable to move elsewhere. Here, you are tying professors to Sardis U by slowly killing their publication records, reducing their options to nothing.

This is even easier on the online side. I was very glad to see that you have had your Subject classify all online faculty and most administrators as "part-time" in order to save money on insurance costs. Now that you've done that, have the administration begin to make essentially full-time demands on their lives. For example, while the professors are paid for teaching part-time, make it clear that they are expected to be on-call all day, every night, and on weekends. They should keep receiving those wonderfully smarmy provost's office communications reminding them just how much they are appreciated and how Sardis wants the best for them, while in the next breath hinting at the expectation that they will enthusiastically *comply* with the very reasonable requirement that all faculty put their lives on hold at 8pm every night of the week to check email (if they don't want their children to be sleeping under a bridge), just to be sure that students don't have to wait until the next morning to have a quiz reset. Since a part-time salary isn't enough for any reasonably-sized family to live on comfortably and still pay for their own medical coverage, life insurance, etc. out-of-pocket, most of these faculty will naturally be forced to take other jobs. You should then have the administration constantly harangue them about it, emphasizing that SCU's part-time work must be treated as more important than everyone else's part-time work (something we'll be emphasizing at the other schools too), heightening the stress and further grinding the insult into the injury. If you follow it all up with more talk of the "team," the "ministry," our "loyalty," and excessive blathering about "how much SCU appreciates you" as it pounds them into the ground, I believe the results will be most satisfying. In short, you want your Subject to force his employees to choose each day between spending time with loved ones and keeping his or her supervisors at SCU happy. You want those supervisors to be keenly aware of how unfair all this is, but to be forced to participate in order to ensure the provost's office is satisfied. And you want those in the provost's office to spend their time in a tizzy of self-importance or, better yet, fearful activity in search of something "progressish" enough to keep your Subject pleased.

The last thing on their minds should be the Enemy.

Yours Infernally,

Wrackturn

-16-
The Importance of *Compliance*

My Dear Nobshank,

I used the word "compliance" my last letter. I even italicized it for you. Imagine my surprise when I noted you did not once mention it in your reply. That sort of obtuseness is simply unacceptable. We'll have to schedule some more professional development. Since you obviously underappreciate the usefulness of such a sublime concept, I shall spend this letter explaining it to you in excruciating detail—though perhaps not so excruciating as our trainers from the Coordinator for the Advancement of Fiendish Excellence will.

In a very real way, compliance plays a central role in what you are foisting onto SCU. It is the deliciously evil twin of the Enemy's old and horrifically regressive concept of servanthood. Often, the results attained by both are very similar: the job gets done. But the key difference is how it gets done and the spirit in which the deed is accomplished. Servants (in the sense of the word the Enemy uses) give of themselves freely in pursuit of His goals, and this often involves quite a lot of trust on both sides. Compliance, on the contrary, is forced upon someone from the outside artificially and inflicted via direct threats. Never make the mistake of treating "servant" as an actual synonym for "slave." While slaveholders have traditionally tried to soften the moral impact of slavery by intentionally confusing the two, in reality a true servant serves by *choice*. A slave complies through fear. Remember, the last thing Our Father Below wants is a "servant." We are his slaves, and that is what we strive to create in others...especially those at SCU.

So, how do you ensure compliance? The first step is to require uniformity. This, as we've noted, is often difficult to do in a university setting where the fools prattle on about "initiative," "originality," and "academic freedom." Thankfully, back during the Americans' "Progressive Era" (more on that word later), we sowed the seeds of a very useful concept we called the "Gospel of Efficiency." This is the idea that everything should be managed by trained "scientists" with dictatorial powers. These specialists took over everything: politics, conservation, agriculture, art, business, and, of course, education. Their goal was to act as secular social engineers, to maximize the productivity of everything they touched while suppressing any wasteful "inefficiencies." Educationists (we can't, in point of fact, call most of them teachers in a meaningful sense) very quickly swallowed this and thus began the slow, systematic corruption of the Western school systems. We've made excellent progress since then, so much so that in the United States, their high schools have gone from expecting students to write in Latin and Greek to graduating those who barely speak English and are functionally illiterate.

Note, of course, that we allowed the schools to continue to teach the Enemy's rot for a time. It was the method and the philosophy that we wanted to establish. Once it was on a solid footing, it was a simple matter to make new rules and require everyone to come into compliance. Since about their year 2000, we have broadened the expanse of compliance to also include colleges and universities. SCU has bought into this more than most, and therefore you can encourage your Subject to promote our agenda and require compliance with whatever rules his people feel fit to publish. Isn't the irony scrumptious? Leave it to the meatbags to let the theories that ruined one educational sphere take control of another! I am not suggesting, of course, that you have your Subject dirty his own hands with this. No, his chosen instrument should be his provost. It really doesn't matter who it happens to be. Any yes-person will do. At SCU, the provostship should really be a disposable position to be occupied by the scapegoat *du jour*. Make the provost your Subject's hatchet man on campus. He non-renews people, axes programs, bullies everyone about compliance, and of course keeps chanting those thinly-veiled threats to the faculty about the people lined up from here to Hell and halfway back, all more qualified than they are, and all pitifully eager to do their job for half the pay. As much of a tyrant as he may be to the faculty, to your Subject he should be a complete sycophant. The dueling expectations should drive people toward schizophrenia. To those below him, the provost's job is to enforce compliance and make the faculty pretend to like it, to make them think Sardis really values them, notwithstanding the bit about how they can be replaced at any local dollar store. To those above him, he must be visibly bowing and scraping and kowtowing, all with a smile and a "God bless you."

Luckily, provosts are a renewable resource. The more the provost does this dirty work for your Subject, the more everyone comes to hate every single inch of the provost's intestines (or at least, they feel sorely tempted to do so). Then, when he's been used up, have your Subject fire him and replace him with a fresh one. The poor sots in the trenches are overjoyed because they blame the departing tool for everything that went before, rarely suspecting the true author of their misery. The wonder is only that your Subject can persuade someone else to accept the job of provost. Well, P. T. Barnum was a pessimist, and greed springs eternal.

I expect to see more about compliance from you, particularly in your provost updates. It will be in your best interest to...ah...well, you know.

Yours Infernally,

Wrackturn

P.S. One of their performance groups has given us a wonderful depiction of how your Subject's provost's office should relate to your Subject. What are they called? Harry Python and the Philosopher's Circus? That is not right. At any rate, go to the infernet and look up the Dirty Fork Skit. They call it comedy. I call it a model of ideal meatbag behavior.

-17-
Proper Propaganda

My Dear Nobshank,

Ah! It is good to hear about the progress you've made with Human Resources. I especially appreciate the fact that you have also made it inefficient and top-heavy. I saw via infernal messaging that it can take up to two years for a "fast-tracked" resume with "connections" to make it through the hiring process! Excellent. Everyone is miserable! Well done indeed. But I do not see where you are increasing your propaganda efforts alongside. This is an oversight that must be righted immediately or you may undo much of what you have gained.

The issue is that while the little meatbags are gullible, selfish, gluttonous, etc., etc., they are not all stupid. Therefore, if you don't give them a "good" reason for why they're being punished, they will start to ask questions. The purpose of a good propaganda arm is to keep everyone satisfied as to why things are the way they are. So, if a person is miserable, you can keep him or her in that state for much longer if you can make them believe that it makes sense for them to be that way (i.e., "I deserve it," "It's for the cause," "Times are bad," etc.). If a person looking in from the outside sees someone else who is being abused, they will ignore it if you can convince them that there is a "reason" for it or, better, that it really isn't happening at all. So, as you magnify the mistreatment, you should also be increasing the output of your propaganda department.

The key to leveraging good propaganda is in understanding what it is. Propaganda is about creating an illusion of reality and then presenting that as actual reality. It tells people what is possible rather than what is true. In a very real way, this is a direct assault on the stronghold of the Enemy and a glorious reaffirmation of Our Father Below. We transform the truth into a lie by bending it to our practical will.

Of course, you probably won't get away with opening a "Ministry of Truth" or a "Propaganda Office" as such just yet, but I think you'll find that a pair of already existent departments will do just as well: Marketing and IT. When we began the big push into online learning, we created a Marketing Department to shill the courses and an IT department to manage the massive network necessary to implement them. In practice, you will find that there is very little difference between what these two departments do and old-line propaganda. Their goal is twofold, and they often work hand-in-hand: to convince students to buy courses at all costs, especially courses they don't need, and to manage the university's image in cyberspace, particularly through social media. All you're doing is broadening the scope and letting them apply their craft not only to the student/customer, but also to faculty, staff, and the wider world. In all cases, they will be using a little truth to sell a lot of lies...just as we like it. More on that later, perhaps.

For now, the possibilities are endless. Internally, you can have them create something like the "You're Important" campaign. They'll print out flyers, paint murals, hand out cute little coffee cups emblazoned with the slogan. They should send out an email newsletter that no one will open filled with smiling faces telling everyone how happy they are to be there. Give out "rewards" like family football tickets to the worst game of the season (the one they know they can't sell tickets to), along with $5 vouchers for $10 hotdogs. This should have most excellent effects. Some of the more naive employees will take these scraps as proof that the university really appreciates them, and they'll take more abuse with less complaint. The more seasoned employees will see this for what it is and be outraged by the thinly-veiled hypocrisy. That will tempt them to all kinds of sin, of course. Finally, the administration will take any attempt to point out the obvious fact that this is just going through the motions as further proof of just how ungrateful the faculty are.

And then there are the university's interactions with the outside world. Here again you have a brilliant opportunity to really drill down into a veritable wellspring of hypocrisy. You should have your Subject's people working to cultivate two completely different images of the university. On the one hand, they should pander to their little Christian Conservative niche by slapping out-of-context Bible verses onto everything and trumpeting their institutional history. On the other hand, they should present themselves to the larger secular world as unreligiously as possible. No references to the Enemy, but lots of blather about "achieving goals," "being your best," "Winners are We," and whatnot. The goal is to have them essentially lie to everyone at once. The Christians are fooled into thinking the main goal of the school is to spread that nauseating "gospel" of the Enemy when the real point is to make money. The secular students are fooled into taking a string of milquetoast "religion" and "Bible" courses that, while we can't make them fully devoid of all truth, will offend them and confirm many of their stereotypes. This will have the added benefit of giving them the false impression that they've "already seen that and it's a croc", when in fact they've seen nothing at all.

And this need not be passive. Remember, you can go farther by spreading outright lies through plainly deceptive means. For example, the social media team can create lists of fake profiles on various platforms. These should then be used to influence polls, troll critics, pack article comments sections with false responses, etc., all in an attempt to influence opinions in the most convenient direction. If you see anyone with qualms about the morality of all this starting to bubble to the surface, just tell them that lying isn't a sin if it's done anonymously on the internet in support of a "good" cause.

Above all, don't let any real understanding of the administration or its treatment of its people leak into the outside world. Everything is awesome. Everything is great when you're a part of the…. You get the picture. And yes, they will buy into it.

Yours Infernally,

Wrackturn

P.S. I was thinking about the "student/customer" combination. As an experiment, suggest to your Subject that they begin calling them "custudents." If you are successful, it will not only give us a good idea of your progress, it will result in many a good chuckle all through the lowerarchy.

-18-
Hell's Motto

My Dear Nobshank,

I see from your comment that your devils have everything "well in hand" that you seem to think you can let them stand pat. Obviously, you do not fully understand the role of "progress" and how to make use of it. Allow me to enlighten you.

As you know from your time in the Tempters University, "progress" is very much essential to all we do in Hell. If Hell had a motto, you can be sure the word "progress" would be in it somewhere. You can see it in the very first real idea Our Father Below conceived so long ago in the dawning of the void. Why should I have to be content with servanthood? Why could I not progress into something more? You can use the word "evolve," if you like, but the essence is the same. We in Hell are always challenging convention, breaking out of molds, remaking ourselves, etc. Constant striving from old to new is part of what makes us who we are!

Progress is also an essential tool in our war against the Enemy. He wants His people to discover and settle into eternal truths that never change. Of course, the fact that they are finite creatures exploring the depths of infinite realities gives them a disgustingly false impression. They believe they are also constantly growing and deepening themselves, yet somehow resting, resting like a tree sinking roots into a thick, loamy soil. So unlike the hard, dry, courageous exhaustion that undergirds so much of our own existence! It is enough to turn the stomach of any reasonable tempter!

Your goal should be to recreate the progressivism of Hell in as many departments of Sardis University as possible. To make that happen, you need to impress upon your Subject the idea that progress is to be valued and even idolized for its own sake. Progress shouldn't be seen as moving *toward* anything in particular so much as *away* from wherever they happen to be at that moment. No matter what they achieve, it should never be enough. The perceived target must always be in motion, one step out of reach.

This is useful to our cause in three primary ways. First, preventing the meatbags from settling anywhere has the pleasing effect of progressing them away from anything the Enemy truly values. The moment they come near some such thing, all it takes is a subtle suggestion to send them spinning off again in a random direction. Which direction really doesn't matter, as long as it is away from that particular point. You may for a while find that you must swing your Subject back and forth over an ideal like a pendulum, but with time and skill, you'll soon have him orbiting it: going round and round in constant motion but never getting any closer.

Secondly, instilling this idea of constant "progress" will result in the most entertaining problems and inefficiencies. They will sometimes find processes and systems that work disgustingly well. Common sense would dictate that the best course of action would be to employ such a process or system consistently until they have a clear need to do something different. But once you have instilled this idea of progress-for-its-own-sake, they will continually upset their own delicate balance without any further effort on your part. Whatever system they have, they'll break it. Whatever process they create, they'll discard it. Often, when they do, they will also discard the people who created it for them. Sometimes you might encounter individuals imaginative enough to survive a culling or two, but eventually they'll all fall from favor and be trampled underfoot in the drive for the next "rock star." You'll get a fine crop of betrayal and hatred on the side, if you're quick to catch it.

Finally, and perhaps more importantly, the meatbags do not have the same infernal stores of energy from which we draw here in the lowerarchy. While the Enemy will sometimes sustain them supernaturally when they are pursuing His will, He generally will let them come to the end of themselves when they are relying on their own strength (which will happen if they idolize progress in place of Him). The result is that the relentless pursuit of progress literally wears them out. They never get any rest, and it isn't long before grinding, marrow-sucking exhaustion sets in. That kind of weariness is all-consuming for them, and it leads directly to a host of deadly sins: wrath, sloth, and gluttony are just a start.

Progress! It's what Hell exists for. Make your Subject love it!

Yours Infernally,

Wrackturn

-19-
Research: Thinking Inside the Box

My Dear Nobshank,

I see from your latest that Sardis is instituting a new university-wide research initiative in response to the prompting of their accreditation agency and in search of grant money. I also see that you have done nothing at all to discourage this. That is very bad. I should wonder what you are thinking. We must act quickly before this pestilence is allowed to spread.

The problem with research is that it encourages original, independent thought. That is absolutely the last thing you want to have happening around SCU! We have worked very carefully over the years to create an imperial atmosphere. Everything thus far has been top-down, and that should include thinking as well. We want a situation where your Subject's own mindset is imposed on his employees and anyone who does not fall into line is punished and belittled. If you allow the faculty freedom of thought, even in areas that seem completely disconnected to anything important, you are permitting them to practice a very dangerous craft. For example, an original thought regarding, say, the use of spiritual themes in Hunger Games by a literature professor may not seem to be any threat to your control of the university, but the very fact that they are thinking at all is what is significant. In order to get published, the scholar must venture outside what they call "the box." If he or she will think outside of that box, what's to stop them from thinking outside of yours?

The good news is, though, that it should be relatively easy to salvage the situation. Your goal should not be to ban all research. Sardis, after all, is a university and just having your Subject declare all scholarship off-limits would be too much for all but the thickest Newritch family fanboy to handle. No, we'll come at this as we have so much else: from the flank.

First, you should seek to make meaningful research as difficult as possible for the average faculty member. Begin with an appeal to the university's pocketbook. The basic math is very simple. If a faculty member publishes a scholarly book, he or she may eventually make enough money to take his or her family out to dinner, and the university won't make anything at all. On the other hand, if the same faculty member teaches a class of 100 students at $815 per residential credit hour, he or she will earn the university $244,500 by the end of the semester. Given that the faculty salary is what it is, he or she has paid his or her own salary four times over in one class. It should be very easy to make the case to any number of university officials on the basis of greed using these numbers. Pack on the teaching hours! Justify it by blathering about SCU being a "teaching university" that "focuses on loving its students." Five classes per semester is a good target (six, if you can manage it), along with required summer teaching. That should exhaust them sufficiently and any time left over should be swallowed up by committee work, student clubs, college preview weekend, etc., etc. Don't stop there! Suggest that more money can be saved by having those lazy faculty do their own grading instead of hiring teaching assistants. Require constant training over Christmas and summer breaks. "After all," you can say, "we can't have them always on holiday!" All of this will effectively end their opportunities to accomplish anything like research or writing, especially if they have families.

This is a fundamental misunderstanding that many university administrators hold that you should encourage at all costs:

specifically, that a professor's sole responsibility is teaching and nothing else. This makes it much easier to ignore the hours put in elsewhere and to look at the actual teaching load and presume that is also the *working* load. Five, three-hour classes is only fifteen hours a week! Surely they can do much more than that! Even better, the fact that over the years many faculty, especially those with tenure, have indeed terribly abused the system in their favor makes this lie very easy to believe.

I expect that you won't be able to completely shut down faculty thinking and research. It's in the blighters' DNA, and there are always one or two that will manage to do it. In such cases, what can't be prevented should be controlled. You want to make it very clear that certain kinds of research and writing—your kind of research and writing—will be rewarded and encouraged, while all else will be punished in some way. This is more easily accomplished than you might think, and you can do it via the initiative you have already let slip by you. Encourage all faculty to apply for time off and for research funding for their interests. Then, curtly deny the ones you don't like while generously endowing those that will further your own agenda.

Of course, you will have seen what we are doing here. I said before that you should be worried that creative, independent thought could train them to challenge your "box." If you should succeed in directing their thought as I suggest, what you are doing is giving them the illusion of independent thought with none of the power thereof. They will crow and trumpet about how they are challenging convention. They will preen and prance, giving each other awards to be hung in their cubicles (I still savor the sweetness—faculty in cubicles) while telling each other how smart and groundbreaking blah, blah, blah, blah. And all the while, they'll remain ignorant of the larger truth that they are contained safely inside the walls of a much bigger box they don't know is there.

Your final defense is to have the school take credit for whatever the faculty produce. In fact, you can write it into their contracts that work created while in the employ of the university, any at all, belongs to the university and must be credited to the university. This will have the most wonderful effect on the faculty who have somehow persevered to publish the study or write the book in the first place, in spite of everything the school has done to stop it.

Yours Infernally,

Wrackturn

-20-
Fear and Entitlement

My Dear Nobshank,

I can see from your somewhat immature comments about using fear to control and influence faculty behavior that you apparently have a...shall we say...underdeveloped understanding of fear. "Incomplete" might be another way of putting it. In either case, it betrays an unacceptable failure to master fear and leverage it. Let us see about correcting that.

You seem to think that fear mostly comes from its victims being afraid of something being done *to* them. This is what you might call a classical conception. It is the fear that the government will persecute you, that your neighbor will murder you, your boss will cheat you, etc., etc. This is bold and primal fear at its most raw. Something is out *there* and it is coming *here* to get *you*. This is a viable and useful form of fear, though perhaps not as useful to us as it once was. So, don't think I'm suggesting that you neglect that kind of fear by any means.

Still, to stop there is old-fashioned. This kind of fear was our primary motivation in more primitive societies. As they "mature" and advance technologically, they begin to develop comforts, and comforts quickly become addictions. Addictions, in turn, lead to a sense of entitlement. Now the person isn't just afraid of the things that will be done, but also of things that won't. I won't have my time to myself. I won't eat that gluttonous meal. I won't go on that vacation. I won't get that toy. I won't make that extra money, and so forth. Better, while the old kind of fear always risks provoking courage, this fear is more likely to invoke a sense of indignant self-righteousness at not getting his or her "due."

What does all of this have to do with a university? The fact that so many people are living as "customers" in what they call an "Ivory Tower," sequestered from reality and expectant of a broad range of comforts, means that they already have been nurtured toward a whole raft of addictions. The faculty are no different. Your main question should be how best to exploit that bent. You want to set up a university-wide system that breeds addictions of all kinds and consequently the fear that one day they may be withdrawn.

You are already off to a good start, given the groundwork we've laid in faculty contracts and working environment. The year-by-year "renewal" process keeps them in constant fear of losing their livelihood and the comforts attached thereunto. But we can go further via the offer of "overload" hours. For full-time positions, this will take the form of classes taught over and above the full-time minimum load they are required to maintain. For each class, you'll pay them extra; the amount itself doesn't matter, just so long as it is enough to be tempting. If they can carry enough of it, they can substantially boost their salaries. A year or two of regular overload and you'll have the faculty accustomed to living far beyond their means and enjoying comforts that they otherwise wouldn't be able to afford. This has a number of excellent effects. First, taking regular overload means that the faculty will almost always be working beyond full-time hours. Given that they have no more hours in their week than before, either they will skimp on their current classes and/or their research (to make it all fit into forty hours), or they will sacrifice family and personal time (leading to stress at home and a lack of personal care). Either decision suits us. Second, it directly affects every interaction the faculty will have with the administration. It will take only the merest hint of disapproval by an administrator or supervisor to make faculty hearts skip a beat. Displeasure means less overload, and less overload will mean curtailing their children's education, canceling that trip to Disney, no vacation, no new car, losing their overpriced home, and so forth. It is even easier to manage this with the online adjuncts. They are far more dependent on that load to feed their families and to pay for healthcare, even if they are carefully guarding every coin.

Applying this sort of fear to the students is no trouble at all. Again, you'll find the groundwork already laid when we created customers instead of servants. You should now further that divide by pulling them in two different directions. First, you want to have your Subject use SU's campus and customer service vehicles to create in the students a completely unrealistic expectation for life. Everything they want, they should have now and they should be exposed to as many creature comforts as humanly possible (more on this in my next missive). This should happen to such a degree that they come to see even a mild deprivation as a "hardship" and "unfair." Done right, you can poison their whole future right here and right now.

But don't stop there! Remember, customers exist for one reason: to have things sold to them. You want to create in the students, as much as possible, an addiction to degrees and completing them. "Why stop with an Associate of Arts when you can get a Bachelor of Science? Why settle for a Bachelor of Science when you can have a Master of Arts? Don't you know the Master of Arts is the new Bachelor's Degree these days? What you really need is a doctorate. The best job candidates are the most flexible. Shouldn't you have an MA in literature to supplement that PhD in computer science?" The combinations are endless...and expensive. You can saddle pastors of meager income with tens of thousands of dollars of debt, scuttle their ministries preemptively, and overwhelm them with a constant feeling of failure because they are not enjoying the absurdly high living standard they experienced in school. That will spill over nicely into all their relationships.

If a man or woman must be a Christian at all, a whining,

disaffected, and unhappy one will have the greatest impact on others for our side.

Yours Infernally,

Wrackturn

-21-
Theme Park U

My Dear Nobshank,

I would now like to shift our attention more fully to what we should expect from the educational vomit...I mean, the products of Sardis University. We have already established the principle that students should be customers, not servants, and we said that you should encourage the leadership to create an atmosphere in which their customers are mined for money like mountains for minerals. You must never lose sight of the fact that, though young, they are very observant and very many enter Sardis with a sincere dedication to the Enemy's cause. You must deaden their senses and reasoning abilities if you want to keep them from waking up to your program. The way to do that is by creating an "opiate" for your people. You will turn SU into the world's first theme park with its own university.

Now, I say "world's first" in sarcasm because, as you well know, the larger trend is something that we are promoting all across the hapless West. It is yet another side effect of students as consumers, schools as businesses, and education as a cash crop. There are two major types of products in this particular market, and they often overlap. The first and most obvious of these products is a degree. You are selling a collection of classes that, when purchased as a set, will qualify a graduate for something. The other product is an experience. Since the end of their Second World War, Americans have come to see college as a strange combination of "rite of passage" and "four-to-six-year-long bachelor/ette party." It is supposed to mark the transition into adulthood by (this somehow makes sense to them) allowing the child-adult to embark on a mostly unsupervised period of near-complete irresponsibility, all paid for by parents and/or the state. Colleges and universities now also surreptitiously compete with each other over who can offer the most complete and thorough opportunity to practice debauchery while still ensuring survival and a chance to earn money when it is all done. This experiential product is your opiate.

Of course, SU will have to approach their "debauchery" a little differently. There will definitely be some legitimate benders, and you can easily encourage the administration to wink at them, but you won't be able to openly market it like some schools do. Instead, you want to create what amounts to a four year "Christian" youth camp. You need constant talk about vaguely "spiritual" topics and loud, blaring, pounding music. Give them food. Give them crafts. Take them on nature hikes. Show them movies. Bring out the puppies, even, if you can stomach it! The goal is to keep them constantly entertained—to death, even.

Note, of course, that none of these things are in any way inherently advantageous to our side. In fact, the Enemy in His inexplicable and disgusting desire for the meatbags' good actually wants them to enjoy all these things and more. I am told He even smiles when He sees them doing so! The eternal stoic decorum of Hell stands outraged at such an indignity! What we want, though, isn't simply for the students to enjoy well-earned recreation at the end of a long day. We want them to see it as an end in-and-of itself and their studies—indeed, the Enemy Himself—as a distraction from it. Best case, we want them to worship their entertainment.

The one place where you can openly compete with secular

schools is in size and sheer avarice. If other schools have walking trails, you can buy a park. If other schools have a coffee bar in the cafeteria, you can bring in Koffee King to every major building on campus. Build bowling alleys and movie theaters. Expand the student center tenfold and add swimming pools and climbing walls and gaming centers. Instead of dorms, offer luxury flats.

What does any of this have to do with education? Everything...from our perspective. With the student body so well distracted with "Christian"-themed entertainment, it will be very easy to convince virtually all the students that your consumer-Christianity is both valid and "deep." It will distract them from whatever truth they may happen to encounter in their classes. As with the faculty and overload pay, it will addict them to their comfort first and foremost. The fear of having that comfort disturbed will increasingly become the prime determining factor in many a life.

Perhaps even better, as we've discussed, it will accustom them to an unreasonably high standard of living and personal attention. These people, who have moved so recently from their mothers' apron strings, will be asked to step forward upon graduation into a very uncertain world to begin over again, often from scratch. They will start jobs where they are not only not the privileged consumer, they are the lowest rung on the ladder. They won't be able to afford the standard of living you have acclimatized them to, and probably won't reach that height again until they have put in years of hard work, if they ever do. Many will become angry and resentful. Others will go into debt to try to maintain an illusion of wealth. More than a few will manage to do both at the same time. Some will attempt to become "missionaries." We'll weed most of those out via student loan debt. If by chance a few of the little worms somehow manage to sneak through debt-free and are accepted into a missionary organization, can you imagine the disappointment when you move them from having their own luxury suite to carrying dirty water up a mountain? Even the very best of them will be sorely tried by that. And all of it comes from preparation on your part. A little entertainment can go a long way, and you'd be surprised at the spiritual mileage we can get out of an amusement park!

Yours Infernally,

Wrackturn

-22-
Breaking the Blank Slates

My Dear Nobshank,

I'm not yet ready to leave my previous topic of students and dealing with them. I think, based on some of your off-hand comments, that you may be in danger of encouraging a sense of hellish realism in the meatbags-in-training. Remember, it is the Enemy's goal to remake them into little putrid versions of Himself. We, on the other hand, don't want to make them like ourselves. We want them as food. For that to happen, we must keep them as far from any view of reality as possible until it wallops them in the face, preferably when they arrive in Our Father's larders. It results in a wonderful sweetening of their anguish!

There is one specific mythology that we have been encouraging in the western democracies that will be of particular use to you here: the idea that "you can be anything if you only try." One of their thinkers once used the phrase "blank slate" to erroneously refer to their moral development. You can consider this the "blank slate" writ large, applying not just to morals, but to everything else. It's the perfect, warm-and-fuzzy poppycock to pour into their heads in this day and age.

Why it's poppycock is obvious to anyone with that sense of realism you should be trying so hard to deny to students at Sardis University. Universal human experience teaches that human beings have different innate gifts and abilities based upon their particular design. For a "healthy" human, part of the process of maturation is a gradual self-discovery, where they learn what they are "good" at and what that can mean for them in their future. There is wide diversity on this point. Some are very good at one thing. Some are moderately good at many things. There is usually some flexibility, and creative humans can make their "one thing" count for several, depending on career choices. It truly is obnoxious. Then there are a few who are very good at just about everything. As these discoveries are made, they all engage as a part of a larger society in order to find the place where they fit and have meaning, allowing for disgustingly endless combinations of what they call "beauty." When it all falls together in just the right way, it is enough to make even the strongest tempter want to vomit.

Anything we can do to disrupt this process is helpful (at least to our stomachs) as we go about our daily chores. As I mentioned above, the line currently most useful is to focus attention on those few geniuses who do all things well, and we make the rest jealous of them. We then spin some lies about "You can do this too! Anyone can be anything!" and our purpose is accomplished. Rather than seek to know themselves, to find their own strengths and become their own people, they spend their lives desperately trying to become someone they're not. When they fail, as they almost inevitably will, at the end of their lives they will die at a confluence of bitter disappointments, staring down resentfully at a bevy of unrealized hopes. This is so much more satisfying to Our Father Below than otherwise!

While we've been feeding them this drivel since birth, university is where it really starts to bear fruit in a serious way. An extroverted person who has a bent toward teaching literature and no aptitude for math may have been convinced that he can be an astronaut or engineer since he was six, but university is where he will first lay down thousands of his parent's dollars to force his way through classes for which he is not adept. An introverted person best suited for books and computers may have always been convinced that she will be president one day and will consider herself a failure at life for anything less...you get the idea. In all cases, we want them slamming their heads against brick walls when they know in their souls that the door is just a meter or two to the right and asking indignantly why they aren't moving forward on their own terms.

Promoting this should not be difficult in your current position. While administrators deep in the Enemy's service may look at this and see a problem to address, our leadership at SU will more probably see an opportunity. Remember, the purpose of the modern university isn't to educate; it's to sell tuition hours. Anything that facilitates more hours sold is a "good" thing in this view. Therefore, while some show of "career services" will be inevitable, you want to put pressure on all the academic departments to swell their numbers in order to justify their existence. This will result in sleek advertising campaigns from the marketing department and pressure from advisers and professors to choose this major or that major. "Choose this one! This job pays the most!" "No! This one! You'll feel the most fulfilled!" "Over here! Ours will let you change the world and be famous at the same time!" Drag the faculty themselves as deep into this process as you can. First, overworked as they are, they will resent having another, non-traditional set of tasks thrust upon them— tasks for which they know themselves to be ill-equipped. If this doesn't promote anger, it should degenerate into depression. Second, when you also make it clear that their jobs depend on the number of majors in each department, it will have a most satisfactory effect of killing what little collegiality might still remain, as professors start poaching students, much like pastors will steal sheep.

The end result is that, rather than soberly taking stock of their abilities and desires and then remaining faithful to a single path, you will have students careening haplessly from one major to the other, and the more often they switch, the better. Remember the idea of orbiting, but never getting closer to an actual, realistic goal? The majors are always greener on the other side of campus, you know! We want to breed into them the idea that since they can be anything, they must settle for nothing. You'll know you've had real success when after seven or eight years, they finally graduate with a multidisciplinary studies degree and decide to sort it out in graduate school.

I think you'll find few better ways to breed discontentment and financial ruin, even in these days of plenty.

Yours Infernally,

Wrackturn

-23-
Christians without Chests

My Dear Nobshank,

I have one more missive for you on the question of studentry, before we move on to other things. In addition to all the other little assignments I've given you, I want you to pay special attention to what I like to call creating "Christians without chests." You will, of course, recognize the wording, reclaimed from that Lewis fellow in his so-called *Abolition of Man* book, where he pointed to our strategy of removing value judgments from human thinking, therefore eliminating morality from their actual practice. Our goal is to continue to erode their sense of right and wrong, especially in the Enemy's church itself. We are therefore attempting to create a culture at Sardis University in which cheating is winked at and dishonesty is positively encouraged by the environment. In many ways, this should flow naturally from your other efforts toward the students. In fact, it can serve as a sort of bellwether for success.

That we could create such a culture of chicanery at a place like Sardis may seem anything but obvious. After all, given that the Enemy cares so much for character and moral values, shouldn't a university dedicated to His service remain equally dedicated to inculcating said values? Given that the Enemy's Abominable Book provides specific step-by-step instructions for excluding people who violate those values and refuse to change their ways, shouldn't such a university take special care to guard its reputation? It would be so, but for our tender ministrations.

Take, for example, the unending greed of various university administrators. We have developed their method of moral discernment into a simple question of "Does this serve to sell another tuition hour or does it place stumbling blocks on the way to it?" How does this affect the issue here posed? Obviously, money paid into university coffers by dishonest people spends just as well as money from honest ones. A student penalized for cheating may decide to transfer to another school, depriving the school of potential income. Therefore, while justifying outright cheating will be difficult, you can certainly "loosen" the definitions and lighten the penalties. The message sent to the customers and the faculty is very clear: there are things worse than lying and cheating, specifically, switching schools.

And do not rule out the possibility of something more blatant, if still unofficial. The administration itself cheats regularly and gets away with it. They've been "creatively double counting" terminal degrees and full-time faculty for the purposes of marketing and accreditation for decades. Shafting their employees has been happening for so long that they now present doing so to the public as a cherished part of university culture (i.e. bragging about "keeping instructional costs low," which is administrative code for mistreating faculty). Then there was that thinly-veiled bribe to the basketball association reported on in the national press, those questionable real estate deals, that sketchy tax filing.... Their creativity when it comes to excusing this kind of thing exceeds our own at times!

The faculty exhaustion you've bred thus far will also aid you here. I've noted with pleasure that the administration continues piling the load higher and deeper and offers less and less in terms of reward. "Part-time" faculty are still tasked with SU requirements every day of the week, year-round. Most have not had a whole weekend off in years and some have not had an actual vacation in a decade. Dealing with cheaters takes time and is emotionally draining, especially when the faculty member expects to be undercut by administrators desperate to keep the students happy at all costs. Worn out by years of punishing neglect, even the most conscientious of faculty may eventually decide it just isn't worth the fight and pass cheaters along.

We are beginning to see some real fruit from our efforts. Hold true to the vision just a while longer, and we'll achieve all we've aimed for and more. Christians without chests, scholars without minds, and believers without hearts! All, in practice, missionaries to their culture for Our Father Below.

Yours Infernally,

Wrackturn

-24-
In the World *and* of It

My Dear Nobshank,

I believe we are coming now to the end phase of our campaign of conquest. If we can hold on but a little longer, all will be achieved and we can begin to consolidate our gains. If so, it will become a holding action, like we've so long and so successfully managed at other major universities, and you and I can move on to bigger and better things. We must secure this victory, though. We have another layer of hypocrisy to create, and it has to do with this myth that SU is at odds with the world.

You know the story. It gets repeated often and once, perhaps, it was at least partially true. When the school was first founded, it was intended to be countercultural. It was supposed to go against the flow and, as such, they expected there to be pushback. Even the Enemy's Son has told them as much in His Abominable Book and it is true. We concentrate our efforts most in the places that are attempting to follow the Enemy the most sincerely. For a time, SU did face some persecution because of its beliefs. For example, they were told they could not question the secular evolutionary paradigm, and so they had to change their class structure to satisfy the critics. A clear inconvenience, yes, but we've thus far followed headquarters' directive for the Americans and not exposed them to anything too serious, to avoid provoking a revival action. And you'll see that this approach has its advantages, which you should be exploiting here. You should remember from the Axiom of Truthful Dishonesty, one of the foundational principles taught at the Tempters University, that lies are their most effective when laced with as much truth as possible. In fact, the very best are 99% true and 1% false—the 1 is very easy to lose in the 99 but, constructed properly, the poison of the 1 is all it takes.

That is why you should now be dealing in truth more efficiently and more effectively (note that I do not say more honestly) than their own seminary professors. Your goal, however, is to divert them from a larger fact, specifically that Sardis University now has far more in common with the world than it ever has before. Virtually every benchmark it now sets for itself comes from that world, from its business model to its educational theory. That is the greater truth, our greater truth, and you must do everything possible to prevent them from realizing it. You do this by false association.

For example, you can remind them of those previous instances where they faced discrimination because of their faith and encourage them to assume that since they were once persecuted for their faith, any time they face opposition now, it must also be because of their faith. You can trot out a long line of "institutional memory" to prove your point, diverting them from the fact that in this instance, the problem originated because the administration is trying to illegally dodge the tax bill on a commercial purchase behind the school's nonprofit status. Remind them again of the undoubted truth that they are a business and that they must make sound financial decisions in order to stay open...and then let them use the "we are a business" line to mask every mean-spirited, disrespectful, un-Christlike action any given administrator commits.

This is the time and place to once again invoke your marketing department. It should always be hard at work, pumping out these kinds of partial truths, overwhelming any opposition through sheer volume. Put those fake profiles to good use and flood the comments section on any critical news piece. (I have appreciated the steps forward the chancellor's office has made in the realm of character assassination with some of their recent firings, by the way. Good work there. It will be rewarded.)

Oh, and this should be especially true of hiring practices. Harken back to the days when your Subject's father was rightfully worried about faculty drift towards secularism. Keep people saying, "That will never happen here!" All the while, whisper, "We're a business!" and "We don't need to hire Sunday School teachers; we need to hire effective leaders!" If you can simultaneously prevent them from ever asking why they can't have both at once, you'll find them rushing to fill their administrative ranks with everyone from lapsed believers to disinterested agnostics to godless pagans, all of them out to make their fortune and sample dainties in the Chancellor's Suite at sporting events. Throughout it all, they'll see themselves as brave, suffering martyrs facing persecution for strongly-held beliefs they have in fact abandoned in all but name.

I know I keep harping, but I am very much looking forward to it. I think you'll find that this will produce one of the best vintages of hypocrite we'll have had in several centuries. Once more unto the breach, as one of their poets has said, and we'll close our wall up with their meatbag dead!

Yours Infernally,

Wrackturn

-25-
Wild at Heart, Coarse in Character

My Dear Nobshank,

Excellent, my good devil! Excellent! Everything has fallen into place. It should be our goal to secure at least two generations of students to the service of Our Father Below. Over the next several years, I want you to accelerate your entrenchment and insulation of the current leadership model and its modified legacy.

Now, we really need not do anything new or drastically different. We must simply encourage your Subject and his team to continue along the lines they are already so obediently following. You should further that spirit of unbridled pride we have been so carefully cultivating until it reaches a point where the caesars might have blushed. You've long ago "established" that the university leadership is above the moral laws it inflicts on everyone else, but previously they have at least respected it enough to pretend to obey it. Then, you made appearing to comply with that law a burden too long borne, making them feel like martyrs even as they defied their own God's precepts in secret. Now it should be easy to make them feel an active and even self-righteous disdain for it all. You can be assured that it will show itself for what it is when we need it to.

There is a very fine line we are walking here, but one that your preparation should make tenable. The Enemy doesn't call His people to be simpering pansies or gullible carpets fit only to wipe one's feet upon. He wants to inspire a truer form of confidence than what we ourselves can manufacture and, through that confidence, He offers his followers True Power. I have seen it revealed in His Wrath! It is terrible to behold! We must be very careful that we do not let all this self-love transform itself into that sort of Enemy-like confidence that could undo everything.

We will be greatly aided in this because the western church in general and Sardis University in particular has abandoned its long tradition of Christian, chivalric manhood and replaced it with a poorly adapted knock-off of a Hollywood action movie. We have had some success in convincing them that being "Wild at Heart" somehow also includes "Stupid in the Head" and "Coarse in the Character," the very things that the ideal of Christian manhood has traditionally defied. The *non sequitur* is sweet when you have your Subject thinking that because he has people slow-smoking wild boars on his campus over "Manhood Weekends," his school is providing everyone with a good example of actual Christian manhood, as exemplified by the Enemy's sacrifice itself.

Another important step that this conceit enables is philosophical. We take this step when we literally begin to insert our arguments into administrative mouths to be spouted on command. With a little work, you can train them to attack the very moral positions the school was founded to defend only a few years earlier. With real skill you can have them switching between one and the other on the same day and in the same breath!

This overwhelming arrogance is really the single blind that works on rational people at this point. Anyone with an ounce of humility or a shred of decency will immediately see the hypocrisy involved, and if there is any interest left to still serve the Enemy, there will be an almost overwhelming desire to put a stop to it no matter the cost. The only reliable defense is in the assumption that it "can't be hypocrisy because it is something that I currently want, and I know it is impossible for someone as moral as me to be a hypocrite." Those specific words aren't likely to occur to them, but as long as that is the moral thrust of their thinking, you will be quite safe.

All of this should, of course, be couched entirely in religious language and it should be encased wholly in religious trappings.

The more lip service to religion you can manufacture, the better insulated our desired pomposity will become and the more brazenly the hypocrisy may blossom. For example, with a little prodding, I'm certain you could get them to remove the School of Theology from the center of campus and replace it with the School of Business! While the symbolism of such an act should be obvious, all of this and more is possible with the blinding effects of not just run-of-the-mill hubris, but religious hubris.

One last comment on the whole "manhood" issue: do everything you can to encourage people to pay attention to the "toxic manhood" fad that is going around. It is entirely to our advantage in this case. The idea of "toxic manhood" is largely legitimate. Even a brief review of what passes for manhood in their popular culture proves that it is entirely inane at worst and a positive threat to others at best. The Enemy would like nothing more, I think, than to see that kind of manhood exposed and replaced with something truly awful: a manhood patterned on the behavior of His Son. Remember, though, your Subject and many others think that the somewhat laughable imitation of the popular conception peddled by the American "manly" subculture is "real" Christian manhood. Therefore, any attack on "toxic manhood" is a direct attack on their own self-image, provoking all the convenient illusions of persecution that make them all dig in their heels.

The last thing we want any of them discovering is what it really means to be a Christian man—or woman, for that matter—but that is another topic for another tempter working with a different individual.

Yours Infernally,

Wrackturn

-26-
NOBSHANK!

I have seen him!

The tyme has ccome! I have received word dddirectly froom Our Father Below himself! Our succcess at Sardis University had been such that he has chosen it—chosen me!—to play a key role in this year's upcoming campaign! Oh! The sheer drknss, terrror, and pain that his mere proximity entails! It is anguish likee no other! One that works out deepest fears and than, so unlike the Enemy's vile Light, hides them deep within himself! I hope that you will be eble to rrread what I am writing. I am still ssshaking, even as I tyyype these wrds from the overwhelming effects of his presence and my mind reels. I not wholly shure what I am ssaying. [Here the translation program could make no sense of the text for a page and a half.] Ah mommment....

There. I am slowly mastering myself. Our Father Below has chosen Sardis University as the lynchpin of his upcoming campaign! Our successes are such that he believes they can be foundational to many, many others! We are to found a new association of schools with its own new accreditation process. This means that Sardis is to become the new standard by which an untold number of future schools will be measured. That's right, Nobshank! I am the composer of this symphony! And Our Father likes my music!

The Wrackturn Method

You now see the effectiveness of my method and of my philosophy. Remember when I said that success was somehow foundational to the meatbags' existence? Our success at Sardis University has provoked a wave of envy across the educational subculture. Everyone is looking at what we have accomplished— particularly the amount of wealth we have created—and they are all scrambling for a piece! Even those who can see the general degradation of belief and scholarship we have wrought are forced to take notice. By our success, we are stealing their students and their tuition funds. Reports are coming in from all over of schools patterning their operations after ours and even administrators intentionally echoing our language when dealing with their faculty and their "customers." Some are stealing from us wholesale! It is wonderful. Those schools will then, in turn, become virtual factories for our sort of thinking and believing!

What we are doing now is simply formalizing the arrangement and making it more thorough. Whereas before the copying was haphazard and unorganized, by creating an association we can make it intentional, and we can enforce our opinions wholesale. It is a further application of our principle of uniformity. Now that we have secured SU, it is our goal to infect as many other colleges and universities as possible with our poison. Even better, this isn't simply an offensive operation. It is equally effective as a defensive measure. By creating a self-reinforcing academic association, we inoculate our conquests from outside criticism by shaping our own standards. Soon, any organization that wants to provide Christian worldview content will need our endorsement, and we can be sure that they set the standards suitably low enough to make everyone comfortable.

And now we see the ultimate beauty and creeping evil of what we have accomplished. What started as a process of undermining the faith of a few measly college students at a school founded in a collection of trailers has become a virus. I used the word "infect" intentionally beforehand, because my ideas have spread far beyond our immediate reach. Perhaps more appropriately, the Wrackturn Method has become a cancer, and we are about to fully metastasize it.

I should like more time, but it cannot wait. It cannot! I shall not write again, at least not for some time. I will be joining you personally at the scene of the coming action. Set up my seat at the top of the bell tower. I'll be able to keep an Eye on all from there. I think I will bring the last little bottle of Caesar medley with me to celebrate our success. I look forward to raising a glass with you to past and future victories—for Our Father Below!

Yours Infernally,

Wrackturn

THE ARISTOCRAT

By G. K. Chesterton

The Devil is a gentleman, and asks you down to stay
At his little place at What'sitsname (it isn't far away).
They say the sport is splendid; there is always something new,
And fairy scenes, and fearful feats that none but he can do;
He can shoot the feathered cherubs if they fly on the estate,
Or fish for Father Neptune with the mermaids for a bait;
He scaled amid the staggering stars that precipice, the sky,
And blew his trumpet above heaven, and got by mastery
The starry crown of God Himself, and shoved it on the shelf;
But the Devil is a gentleman, and doesn't brag himself.

O blind your eyes and break your heart and hack your hand away,
And lose your love and shave your head; but do not go to stay
At the little place in What'sitsname where folks are rich and clever;
The golden and the goodly house, where things grow worse for ever;
There are things you need not know of, though you live and die in vain,
There are souls more sick of pleasure than you are sick of pain;
There is a game of April Fool that's played behind its door,
Where the fool remains for ever and the April comes no more,
Where the splendour of the daylight grows drearier than the dark,
And life droops like a vulture that once was such a lark:
And that is the Blue Devil that once was the Blue Bird;
For the Devil is a gentleman, and doesn't keep his word.

https://www.moralapologetics.com/